# Red Fern Press

**California Love.** Copyright ©
2025 by Steph West. All rights
reserved. Printed in the United
States of America. No part of this
book may be used or reproduced in
any manner without written
permission except in the case of
brief quotations embodied in
critical articles and reviews. For
permissions, address
correspondence to Red Fern Press,
3136 Kingsdale Center, #103,
Columbus, OH 43221.

Red Fern Press books may be
purchased for educational,

business, or sales promotional use.
For more information, please e-mail the marketing department at
redfernpressquery@gmail.com.

First Edition

ISBN 978-1-967038-03-9 (Kindle)
ISBN 978-1-967038-21-3 (Paperback)

The heart can heal, no matter the break.
Don't ever stop believing that.

# Content

# Suggestions for Further Reading

*On Fire* by Steph West (Red Fern Press, 2023)

*Newcross* by Steph West (Red Fern Press, 2024)

## Coming Soon

Book 3 of the *Double Digits* series, *The Pond House*, by Steph West

Book 2 of the *Newcross* trilogy, *Bounty*, by Steph West

# California Love

*Double Digits Pocket Romance Series*

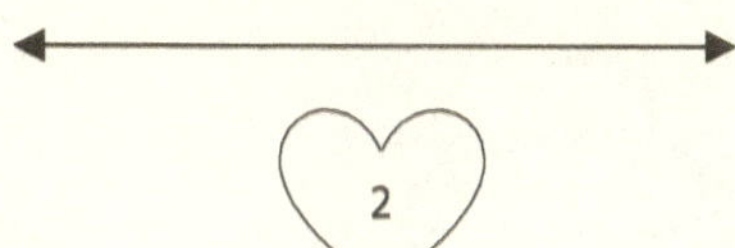

# 1

**Waves of Love**

Scout hopped out of her white Jeep in her and Josh's garage in Del Mar as the door came down on the southern California late afternoon sunshine. She tucked a hair behind her ear before stopping just shy of the entryway into their near three-million-dollar cottage.

"Shoot." She couldn't help being distracted after her doctor's visit and had, for the second time since she left the gynecologist, forgotten her little Chanel pocketbook on the passenger seat.

"Come here." She opened the passenger side door, grabbed the quilted beauty, and turned back to the pristine, white door into the mud room. She held the handle for a moment before steeling herself and walking through it.

The room was bright and sunny, just like the rest of their home, which was a heavenly haven for them in this pristine neighborhood. She immediately heard their golden retriever, Buster, scratching on the other side of the basement door.

"Josh," she muttered under her breath. The door handle of the basement and the garage door into the house were the same model, with a little knob on the handle that locked them. Josh had developed a habit of locking the garage door and absent-mindedly locking the basement door along with it.

"Buster," she said lovingly as she let out the excited retriever. "Did Daddy lock you in the basement again?"

She laughed as his brown eyes happily stared at her and his butt wiggled crazily. He was just under a year old and still considered a puppy. Scout had been looking to get a dog and enjoy the beauty of North Beach—a popular spot for canines and their owners—before Josh had arrived to make their relationship official. Once they decided to move forward, he'd gone with her and helped her pick out the wiggly pooch.

Josh had stayed in a short-term month-by-month luxury apartment for the first few months they dated. But, soon enough, they realized this was, indeed, "it." A month later, when Scout's lease was up, they picked this classic Del Mar cottage together. And, of course, Buster then became Josh's dog, too.

Since then, Scout had spent the last several months of her life in a beautiful bubble. She had never walked lighter, smiled brighter, or felt sweeter. Josh was at the root of all of it. She loved everything about him, about living with him, especially in this place.

Scout loved this neighborhood, especially now, right before Christmas. It reminded her of the close-knit vibe of Pittsburgh, but with better weather. They'd had a couple neighborhood barbeques and a few poker nights. She'd gotten to know some of the girls in the neighborhood and all of them were around the same age, getting married and having babies. All things she and Josh were probably headed for.

"Josh?" she yelled. She walked past the galley kitchen with its stainless-steel appliances and into the dining room with its vaulted ceilings and sleek white dining table. She threw her keys on the shiny surface with a clanking thud. "Baby?"

She paused to listen and heard the treadmill going in the workout room off the side of the house. It was, more accurately, a sunroom that they had made into a workout room. It overlooked their private backyard awash with wisteria.

Josh had taught her about weightlifting, which she really enjoyed. While her curves were still firmly intact, she'd built up some muscles that gave her a nice firm look in her arms. It complemented the delightful curves of her hips and breasts.

She strolled into the tiny room drenched with golden sunlight and grinned as she took in his firm, shirtless body. The sweat ran a wet line from his loose, dark hair and chiseled jaw down his neck onto his toned chest. She felt an immediate heat soar through her body as he finally glanced up at her and smiled his sexy grin.

"Hey beautiful," he said silkily. His dark eyes sparkled as he pulled his air buds out. "Damn, you look sexy."

He stopped the treadmill and jumped off, walking toward her.

"Thanks," she said. He slid his hands around her waist and gripped her as he gave her a deep kiss.

"You taste salty," she said. She licked her lips as she cast a steamy stare at him.

"I'd like to know how you taste right now."

She laughed. "I just came from the doctor. I need a shower first."

She gave him a pouty look as she ran her fingertips down his sweaty, tanned chest. It had just enough hair for her to play with after sex. "You do, too, baby."

"Mmm," he murmured. His hands slid down her back to her bottom and gripped it. "Yes, I do."

He slowly walked her backward as his hands slid up her dress then back down again as he unzipped it.

"Oops," he said. He smiled as he tugged at it, and it dropped to the hardwood floor. "Sorry about that."

She laughed as she tugged on his black gym shorts. They fell to the ground exposing his naked, beautiful body. "Oh, my bad, baby."

He grinned as he paused and took off his shoes and socks. "I don't think you feel bad about that at all."

She unhooked her bra, dropping it to the floor as she slid off her thong.

"Leave your heels on, baby."

She stepped out of her panties and felt her insides respond heatedly to his hardening body. "Whatever you want, baby," she purred.

"Mmm, that view will never get old." He moved toward her in one quick motion, pulling her naked body into his and kissing her deeply.

"Let's go get clean in the shower." He grinned at her.

"Mmm," she moaned. "Yes, lets."

He lifted her up and she wrapped her legs around him as he carried her down the hall to their rain shower for a late afternoon delight.

Scout lightly ran her fingers up
and down Josh's back as they lie
naked together in their King size
bed. The white and cream fluffy
blankets and pillows were starting
to take on a darker shade as the
twilight hour fell upon them. His
hand caressed her chest and
stomach as she smiled lazily.

"I could stay like this forever,"
she murmured.

"Mmm," he sighed. "Forever
sounds perfect, baby."

A jolt of electricity shot through
her as he smiled. He'd been saying
things like that for the last couple
of months. Forever, next steps,
future—she had a sneaking
suspicion he was ready for the next
step. The big one. "Yeah, it does."

Forever with Josh sounded good to her. Living with him only furthered that emotion. Her only concern was that she had never been quite sure about the idea of marriage. Probably her very liberal mother's influence. On the flip side, the romantic in her couldn't help imagining her in a beautiful, white gown and Josh in a tux.

"Buster!" she exclaimed as the puppy burst through the bedroom door with his leash in his mouth.

"Somebody wants a walk before dark," she said as she tapped Josh's back.

"Duty calls," he said lazily. He lifted his head and grinned at her. She gave him a light kiss as he got up and pulled on a pair of briefs followed by loose, navy-blue joggers. They hugged his waist as he slid on a plain T-shirt over his taut muscles.

"You're so sexy, baby," she cooed.

He grinned. "All for you." He slapped his legs. "Come here, Buster."

As he rubbed the dog's head she said, "You locked him in the basement again."

He flicked his stare to her. "Oh damn, did I?"

She nodded. "You've got to either stop doing that or fix it."

"I'll have to change the door handle."

"Isn't there a key?" she asked.

"Oh, you know what, maybe that's what that key is downstairs that I threw in the side table drawer."

She laughed. "Good place for it."

"Right?" He laughed with her. "Oh, hey, how was the doctor, babe?"

She shrugged as she pulled the cozy Egyptian threads around her body and sighed. "It's the gyno. I mean, it's on par with the dentist."

He laughed. "Yeah, I defer to you on that one."

She felt her smile fade as she reached for her lower stomach and held it for a second.

"Baby?" Josh asked concerned.

She shook her head as she pushed out a breath to control the sudden pain in her pelvis. "It's okay."

"It's not okay, I can see that," he said. He walked over and climbed on the bed, touching her face. "Pain again? Your pelvis?"

She nodded as she exhaled, and it started to subside. "It's going away."

"You told the doctor, right?"

She nodded.

"And?"

She shrugged. "Probably nothing. Just bad periods. It runs in my family."

"But you're not on your period right now and you're having pain."

She cast a loving gaze on him. For a minute she thought about telling him that her doctor wanted her to have a laparoscopy. Or, if that felt too invasive, an ultrasound. But she was having a hard time admitting to herself she may have endometriosis. Something that could cause fertility issues. A condition that Josh, who wanted kids, might not want to hear. And she didn't want to raise that red flag until she knew for certain.

"Let me get my test results from the pap and the blood draws and we'll go from there, okay?"

She smiled as lightly as she could until he kissed her.

"Okay," he said. She could tell he didn't quite believe her, but he wasn't going to press it. He climbed off the bed and clapped his hands. "Let's go, Buster."

Josh took the leash from Buster's mouth, and they hustled out the door as she sighed.

She wanted everything with Josh. A lifetime of love, children, memories—everything. The idea she might not be able to give him one of those things was killing her.

She'd wait to tell him. After all, nothing was certain yet. And there wasn't any pressing reason to think otherwise.

She threw the cozy blankets off her, got out of bed, and pulled on some comfy clothes. She'd make him something delicious for dinner and when they woke up in the morning, she'd give him his favorite thing—morning sex.

Anything to keep his mind off her doctor—and her mind off deciding about which test to get, and when to tell Josh.

# 2

## Surprise!

The next morning, Josh stepped into their glass shower with sea-blue tile and couldn't stop the smile from spreading across his face. Making love to Scout in the morning was like a jolt of happiness to start his day, and even more so now that he was certain she was the only one he wanted to do that with for the rest of his life.

"Baby, I'm making breakfast," Scout hollered into the bathroom. "You want pancakes?"

"Yes, please," he hollered back. He glanced through the glass and saw her beautiful curves and long, dark hair turn away as she headed for the kitchen.

"Love you," she yelled as her voice disappeared out of the room.

"Love you too," he bellowed.

He lathered up his body with Sandalwood-scented body wash as he hummed to himself.

He'd bought Scout's ring just after their eight-month anniversary. He had told her he was flying home to Pittsburgh for Double Digits business, but really, he was getting his grandmother's wedding ring from his dad. Lucas had bought his own ring for Jaime, so the diamond had been his for the taking.

He'd gone to a local jeweler and designed it himself, using his grandmother's stone as the centerpiece and building around it.

It was important to him that it be his grandma's diamond anchoring

Scout's ring. His grandparents had one of those storybook loves. And that's how he felt about Scout. He'd never been so certain in his life. The picture in his mind about their life together was crystal clear and perfect.

"Mmm-hmm," he sighed.

The stream of warm water washed the suds down his body and into the drain. He turned his body for one more rinse then shut off the water and jumped out. He grabbed his fluffy blue towel and did a quick rub down before wrapping it around his waist and heading to the bedroom. He was surprised to find Scout there.

"I thought you were makin' pancakes?" He grinned. "Unless you want *me* for breakfast? Again."

He was confused when her eyes shot wide open and a familiar voice yelled, "I'll take the pancakes over you any day, you egomaniac!"

Josh caught his breath as his little brother's sandy-blonde head popped around the doorframe just behind Scout. Both of them were grinning.

"Your brother's here," she quipped as she tilted her head.

"What's up, big brother?" Lucas spread his arms wide as his light eyes sparkled.

Josh couldn't help but chuckle at his little brother's smiling face.

"I'll be damned," Josh said. "What the hell are you doing here, little brother?"

Deep down, Josh already had suspicions about why Lucas was here right before Christmas.

It had happened when Josh went to Pittsburgh for Scout's ring. While he was there, Lucas had dropped not-so-subtle hints that he wanted him and Scout to return to Double Digits. Josh hadn't taken the bait, but in his gut, he knew he wanted that, too. It was the perfect plan for him and Scout after they were married.

The only problem was, he didn't know if Scout would think that was the perfect plan, too. She was happy in California and with her job, and she was damn good at it, too—which is why Lucas wanted her and him back home.

"Get dressed and I'll tell you why," Lucas said. He turned and walked out. "Scout, can I have some of those pancakes?"

Scout raised an eyebrow at Josh. "Did you know he was coming?"

"Nope," Josh said. He did a terrible jazz hands impression. "Surprise."

She laughed as she turned and walked out, shutting the door behind her. "Don't touch my kitchen, Lucas, I'll get you your pancakes."

"Fine!" Lucas hollered from the dining room.

As Josh threw on his board shorts and a T-shirt, he couldn't help but smile that his little brother was here. That was followed quickly by a frown—what if Scout

didn't want what Lucas was likely
here to offer?

And how could Josh tell her that
he did?

Josh stared at his little brother
from across the dining room table
as he reached out and moved the
vase of tall, yellow flowers to the
left for a better view of the younger
sibling chowing down pancakes
drenched in syrup. Even though
Lucas was thirty years old, and just
two years younger than he was,
Josh still felt protective of the
energetic kid who used to follow
him around and beg him to play
G.I. Joe or light stuff on fire.

"Need more syrup?" Josh raised a sarcastic eyebrow.

"No." Lucas grinned as he took a huge bite that dripped melted butter and maple deliciousness onto his blue-striped ceramic plate. Josh was surprised it didn't land on Lucas's red Polo shirt.

"Honey…" Jaime trailed off as she shook her head and smiled warmly at Josh.

He was glad Lucas and Jaime had made the trip together. Josh had always wanted a little sister and Jaime fit the bill perfectly with her blend of sarcasm, wit, and warmth.

She looked the same as when Josh had met her more than a year ago—tall, honey-blonde beauty who fit effortlessly into the

California scene. And yet, something about her seemed different.

"What?" Jaime asked. Her crystal blue eyes drew into questioning slits as she pointed to her forehead and then his. "You're crinkling your forehead."

"Oh, am I?" Josh asked. He shifted in his seat as he lifted his right hand and did a pointed swirl of his index finger at her. "You look different. Did you do something to your hair?"

"I thought that, too," Scout said. She sat down next to Josh with her matching coffee mug and smiled at him. God, he loved her, with those piercing green eyes and warm smile.

"You look extra breezy and happy," Scout commented. "Or maybe that's just because you got R.J. and Katherine to watch Casey for you guys while you're here?"

"Or maybe the newlywed vibe?" Josh glanced at his brother, then at the bright gold band on his left ring finger.

"Probably a little of both," Lucas said. He finally put down his fork and pushed his plate away as he and Jaime shared a secret stare.

"What?" Josh asked. He knew his brother, and he knew that stare. Something was up.

"We're pregnant," Jaime gushed.

"Oh my God!" Scout jumped up as her little yellow sundress flared. She rushed to the other side of the table as Jaime jumped up to meet her. The girl screams were loud as Josh and Lucas grinned at each other.

"Holy shit," Josh said. He leaned forward in his chair, crossing his fingers together as he leaned on the modern, white table. "You're procreating."

"I know, right?" Lucas made his eyebrows dance as they both laughed.

"Ah, little brother." Josh could feel the tears gather at the backs of his eyes as he stood and walked to Lucas, who met him halfway in a half-hug. "I'm so happy for you."

"Thank you," Lucas said. They pulled away with slaps to the arms.

"Growin' up, huh?"

"Just needed the right woman," Lucas said.

"Yeah." Josh glanced at Scout and felt his heart squeeze with happiness. He knew what that meant. To find the right person who just made everything click.

"You're next, huh?" Lucas asked. He glanced at Scout and then back to Josh.

"I hope."

"When are you asking?" Lucas whispered.

"Tomorrow night. One-year anniversary." Josh shoved his hands in his pockets as his chest puffed out. "Taking her to Pacifica Del Mar after I do it. It's a little, intimate seafood restaurant."

"Oh shit, did we ruin it?" Lucas asked surprised.

"Nah, nah, you're good. Maybe take a holiday drive up the coast or something?" Lucas nodded at him in agreement.

"How long are you staying?" Josh asked. "Surely you'll head back before Christmas."

Lucas shrugged. "We will. So, maybe a week? Depends."

"Depends?" Josh asked. "On what?"

His brother's stare confirmed his original inkling of why Lucas was here in the first place. Aside from the baby news, Lucas was here to recruit him and Scout back to Pittsburgh.

"Lucas, Scout is happy at StudioX. I can't ask her to give it up."

"Yes, you can," Lucas said. "I promise. Just give me ten minutes to convince you."

Josh sighed as he peered at his brother. His lifelong partner-in-crime, his buddy. He glanced to Scout—his new partner-in-crime and forever love. He could feel the push and pull. He didn't want to ask Scout to go back to Pittsburgh when he knew how happy she was here. On the flip side, he missed his family.

In his heart, Josh was hoping Scout *wanted* to move back to Pittsburgh after they got married, to raise their family. It wasn't far-fetched—she had, sort of, implied that, too. But implying wasn't agreeing. And he was suddenly aware this was a conversation they hadn't had as a couple, yet, but needed to.

"All I can promise is that I'll let you pitch me," Josh relented. "Do it over jet skis?"

"Jet skis at Christmas? Hell yes." Lucas slapped Josh's arm. "Damn I love the coast."

"Looks good on ya." Josh chuckled.

Scout and Jaime headed over to the boys.

"Honey, we're going shopping," Scout said. "Baby stuff."

"For me." Jaime winked as she touched her stomach, her gray tank top wrinkling under her fingertips. "Lingerie for her?"

"Yes, please." Josh grinned.

"It is our anniversary," Scout said. She sauntered up to Josh and kissed him. Her lips were soft, and he loved the way she tasted. Cherry

ChapStick. She put it on every morning, and it always lingered on his lips until lunch.

"Happy almost anniversary," he whispered.

"You, too, baby." She kissed him again before she ran off to get ready.

His heart swelled as he glanced at Lucas and Jaime talking quietly in their own little world.

Family was everything to him. And he couldn't wait to have his own, too. And, maybe, hopefully, do it all in Pittsburgh, where he and Scout could have everything they ever wanted.

3

## Get It Over With

Scout fingered the clean, pale blue onesie as a strong maternal instinct gripped her gut. The fabric was so soft, softer than anything she'd ever felt. She ran her thumb over the little bear on the front and across the blue stitching that read "Beary Sleepy," as Christmas music played over the mall's loudspeakers.

"It's cute, isn't it?" Jaime walked up beside as her jasmine and vanilla perfume hung lightly in the air between them. "They don't have as many cute things for boys as they do for girls."

Scout looked into Jaime's eyes twinkling with excitement.

"Do you want a girl?" Scout asked as she put the onesie back.

"Desperately." Jaime laughed. "But I think Lucas wants a boy. You know, the first-born to be a son, kind of thing. He's traditional like that."

Scout nodded. She was noticing that about Josh, too. He had a lot of traditional notions, and she could feel he wanted her to feel the same way. Some of it, she wanted, too. Other things, like staying at home, she didn't.

"What?" Jaime asked.

"Huh?"

"You zoned out for a second."

"Nothing," Scout said. She smiled as she shook her head. "When will you know? If it's a girl or a boy."

"Around four months," Jaime said. She rubbed her stomach, which had a barely there bump. "I'm through my first trimester already. You're supposed to wait to tell people until then…you know, things can happen."

Scout nodded. "I've heard that."

"Do you want kids?"

Scout nodded. "So many kids."

They both laughed as a mother walked up and grabbed the onesie Scout had put down, smiled, and walked away to the register.

"Me, too," Jaime said. "So does Lucas. A whole swim team. I told him to dream on."

Scout chuckled. "I would never have guessed that from Lucas."

"People can surprise you." Jaime picked up a pink onesie and smiled.

"He's a great stepdad, too. Casey loves him."

"That doesn't surprise me at all," Scout said as she stepped forward to let a pregnant mom waddle through. "Lucas is young-at-heart."

"So, true," Jaime said. She put the onesie down. "You seem like something's on your mind. Is it work? Thanks, by the way, for taking a few days off while we're here."

"Oh, no problem, happy to do it, and it's expected with the holidays. Not much happening," Scout said. She mindlessly trailed her fingers along the other blue, pink, and white onesies on the shelf. "You know, I guess I didn't realize how traditional Josh and Lucas really

are. I mean, I should have. Paps
was like that."

"I wish I would have known
Paps," Jaime said. "Lucas just
idolized him. Tries to run the
company the way Paps would, you
know?"

Scout nodded. "I do know. Paps
loved that company. A love letter to
his wife. He really believed in it.
The boys do, too."

Jaime nodded. "Are you worried
Josh is too traditional?"

Scout gave a little shrug. "I don't
think so. Or maybe…maybe I do?"

Jaime laughed and Scout smiled.

"That sounds so indecisive."
Scout shook her head. "Josh loves
me. He'd support whatever I
wanted. I think."

"I agree," Jaime said. "Lucas is like that, too."

Scout nodded as she crossed her arms thoughtfully. "And Josh is the guy for me. Like, hands down. He's my person."

"That's obvious. For both of you." Jaime smiled.

"I'm just wondering," Scout said. "I think we both want to go in the same direction. But maybe in different ways? Does that make sense?"

"Are you talking about marriage?"

Scout nodded as she uncrossed her arms and slid her hands into the hidden pockets of her sundress.

"Hmmm," Jaime murmured. "That's a big topic."

"It is." Scout nodded with a little shrug as another pregnant woman slid by.

"Talk to him." Jaime touched Scout's arm. "Forever is a big deal. And how you get there is, too."

Scout nodded. "You won't say anything to—"

"I won't tell Lucas," Jaime interrupted. "Girl talk. Between you and me."

Jaime held her pinky finger up as Scout laughed. She wrapped her own pinky around Jaime's as they squeezed before letting go.

"I'll say this and then I'll say no more," Jaime said. "As someone who was married to the wrong person and divorced. And then married to the right person…when it's right, it's incredibly satisfying.

I mean, it's not perfect, of course. But it's safe and secure and it feels like you have a partner for life, you know? Good days and bad."

"And it never felt like…" Scout paused.

"Felt like what?" Jaime asked.

"Like, institutional? Like, it was some antiquated notion? Or trapped or something?" Scout laughed because she wasn't sure what else to do. As soon as the words came out of her mouth, they felt like her mother's. And she wasn't sure if she owned them or if her mother did.

"Never," Jaime said. "Not to me. But I wanted to be married. I wanted a husband. And I wanted it to be Lucas. And I wanted to have babies and a home and…marriage gives me that. And Lucas wanted me to be his wife and to have kids and have that security, too. Marriage gives *him* that."

Scout gave a weak smile as Jaime touched her stomach again.

"Plus, you know," Jaime said. "Love."

Scout felt her insides contract. Yes, there was that. Love. And she loved Josh more than anyone or anything in her life.

"There is that," Scout said quietly.

Jaime nodded. "I hate to interrupt this but…baby needs to eat. And so does Mommy," she quipped. "Don't you hate it when moms talk like that?"

Jaime laughed at herself as Scout smiled. She loved that about Jaime, how easy going she was and fun to be around. It was probably what Lucas saw in her, too.

"Do you mind if we eat? And we can talk more there?" she asked.

"Not at all," Scout said. She grabbed a few of the plain white onesies and a soft, cream-colored blanket. "I saw you eyeing this."

"No, you don't have to."

"I want to," Scout said. "Let me get this for you guys for Christmas. You head to the food court. I'll meet you there."

"Okay," Jaime said. "I've got my phone. I'll text you where I'm at."

"Perfect," Scout said. She smiled as Jaime walked out of the brightly store into the crowded mall decorated with Christmas lights and tinsel. She took her phone out of her pocket and dialed the doctor's office.

"Hi, this is Scout, I was in yesterday," she said nervously. "I've decided to just go with the laparoscopy. Just get it over with, you know?"

Scout smiled at another pregnant woman who breezed by, and she felt her insides tighten.

"Tomorrow is great," Scout said. "I'll be there."

As Scout hung up and tucked her phone away, she touched her stomach and exhaled a long, taut breath.

# 4

## Upping the Ante

Josh roared up on his jet ski next to Lucas's near the shore of the expansive lake that was about twenty minutes from their home. He brought the powerful machine to a halt as the two brothers laughed together and took in the beach dwellers lying in the sun. Kids were building sandcastles while anxious mothers slathered them in sunscreen.

"We're gonna be just like those dopes." Lucas grinned. Even though his light eyes were covered by sunglasses, Josh was certain they were lit with humor.

"You already are, stepdad," Josh said.

"I love it, man," Lucas said. He grinned at Josh as he sat back and lightly gripped his lifejacket. "I really do."

"I can see that." Josh was proud of the man Lucas had become. The father he was and was going to be. "Jaime and Casey are lucky."

"Nah, me," Lucas said. He tapped his chest. "I'm the lucky one."

A comfortable silence descended upon them as they watched the royal blue waves roll onto the beach as the families splashed in them.

"I miss having you around big brother," Lucas said.

"Miss me kicking your ass at everything?"

Lucas spit out air. "Yeah, right."

Josh grinned. He could always get under Lucas' skin. He had been doing it since they were old enough to walk and talk.

"I'm serious," Lucas said.

Something about his tone caused Josh to look at his brother. "What's going on?"

Lucas sighed. "Look, you know I love Double Digits."

"Yeah," Josh said hesitantly.

"But do you remember growing up? Where we spent most of our time?"

Josh nodded. He knew where this was going.

"We basically grew up inside of Double Digits," Lucas said. "Especially after mom died."

Josh adjusted his sunglasses and wiped water off his legs. They'd had fun in their childhood, sure, but Lucas was right. They only saw their dad and Paps at the company headquarters. They may as well have had beds there.

"I don't want my kids to grow up like that," Lucas said quietly. "I want to be a real dad. You know? Little league. School pick-ups. Bitching with the moms about their husbands."

Josh laughed as Lucas slapped his arm.

"You know I'm good for that conversation with all the hot moms."

"Jaime might kill you."

"Nah, she knows I'm devoted to her." Lucas smiled. "It's not that I don't want the company. Or that I want to dump it on you. I mean, I was dropping some pretty legit hints when you were home a few months ago."

"I picked up what you were puttin' down." Josh raised a haughty eyebrow.

"I know," Lucas said. "I just think we should go back to the original plan. That we should run it together. And by together, I mean, I think Scout should take over as CEO. She's always had the chops. Now she's got the StudioX experience. She's ripe for the position. And I think she'd totally transform the company."

Josh nodded. "I understand that, Lucas, but what about when she and I have our own kids?"

"What do you think? She's gonna stay at home?"

Josh shook his head in surprise. "I mean."

Josh had to pause. No, Scout wouldn't stay at home. Of course he knew that. But for some reason, in his mind, when he pictured their family life, he always saw her at home with their family. Like his mother, who had owned an art studio that took up some of her time, but never more than her children.

"Scout is always gonna work, Josh," Lucas said. "It's in her. And she's great at it."

"Yeah, I mean," Josh muttered. "Yeah. Of course."

"And when you all have kids, I mean, I'll still be there, too," Lucas said. "I'm not going away. I'm just saying. I want more balance. For my family. And I really want you to come back. I want my kids to have their uncle, you know? Right now, they're getting way too much R.J."

Josh had to laugh at that. It was never good to have too much R.J. He was a good man, but he was a little much sometimes.

"So, what are you proposing exactly?" Josh asked.

"Well, I'd like Scout to take over as CEO," Lucas said. "Do you agree?"

"I do," Josh said. Josh had always known that Scout would be perfect to lead Double Digits. True, she needed that C-suite experience at a place like StudioX, but she'd gotten that. She was a rock star. "You know StudioX won't let her

go without a fight. She also has a
one-year, non-compete clause."

"Yeah, I figured," Lucas said. He
smiled at Josh.

"Shit," Josh said. He shook his
head. "You want me to run it with
you during Scout's non-compete
year. Then Scout takes over and—"

"You take over the Foundation,
which is what you love, and I move
into the COO role."

"Well played, little brother."

"I have my moments." Lucas
grinned as the waves gently rocked
them under the California sun.
"Well, what do you think?"

Who was Josh kidding? He
loved it. And he knew that Lucas
knew that he loved it. The question
was, would Scout love it?

"I'll talk to her," Josh said. "But I can't guarantee anything, you know that?"

"I get it," Lucas said. "I'd just really like to have you back, that's all."

A quiet moment settled between them.

"I need my big brother," Lucas said quietly.

Josh's chest squeezed as he gave a sidelong glance to the younger Janssen. "Yeah, I guess I miss having you around, too."

Lucas grinned. "Yeah, you need someone to knock you down a peg."

"Okay, whatever."

"Let's take another round, huh? Then head back?" Lucas started up his jet ski as Josh followed suit.

"Yep, let's do it," Josh agreed.

As Lucas took off and Josh fell in line beside him, Josh could feel joy bubbling up, but also uncertainty.

What if Scout didn't want this, too? What would he do then?

He gave the jet ski gas and roared along the waves as the sun warmed him and his brother under the California sky.

## 5

## Will You?

Scout's eyes fluttered open the next morning to bright sunshine streaming through large skylights into her and Josh's cozy, warm bedroom. She glanced to her left and a smile spread across her face. There, on her side of the comfy bed, was a single red rose with a note.

*Happy anniversary, baby. I love you. Love, Josh*

She held the note to her heart as she took a deep breath and thought about the last year with him. Scout had never expected to find "the one." The notion had seemed relatively silly to her, as did fairy tales and prince charmings. Or maybe that was her mom talking again?

All Scout knew was that when she ran into him at Double Digits—literally—and spilled coffee all over him, she knew. Something in her gut spoke loudly to her heart that this guy was it. And he really was *it*.

"Hey gorgeous," he said smoothly as he walked in with a wooden tray filled with breakfast and coffee. He looked so sexy in his loose joggers and no shirt, his hair rumpled and messy.

"Hey baby," she said. She slid up the bed into a sitting position as he put the wooden tray down across her legs before climbing in next to her.

"Happy one-year anniversary,"
he said. He leaned over and kissed
her gently.

"Happy one-year anniversary,"
she replied quietly. "I love you,
Josh."

"I love you, too, baby," he said.
He ran a finger down the side of
her face and kissed her again.
"Excited for our date tonight."

"Me, too," she said. She took a
sip of her coffee and flashed her
eyes at him over the edge.

"God, you're beautiful."

She swallowed her coffee and
grinned. "Stop that."

"Nope," he said. He grabbed
some strawberries from her tray
and ate them voraciously. "I have a
Zoom meeting with the Foundation

and then I need to edit my photos and get them ready for the studio."

"The one of the mountains is my favorite," she said as she put her coffee down and started into her French toast.

"Yeah, right?" He nodded. "Me, too. Sun was just right."

She nodded as she grabbed another big bite. Good Lord, the man could cook.

"This is delicious," she said with a full mouth. He laughed and grabbed a few more strawberries before giving her a quick kiss and hopping out of bed.

"I need to get moving," he said. As he dressed for the day, he glanced at her. "Lucas and Jaime are driving up the coast and staying overnight at an Airbnb. So, they'll be gone until tomorrow afternoon. Are you gonna go into the office at all today or…?"

"Oh, I'm totally off for the holidays," she said. She grinned at him. "Plus, I feel like I won't get much sleep tonight, so I'll need the day off."

She winked at him, and he laughed.

"Damn straight, you won't get any sleep, sexy." He gave her a sultry stare.

"But, uh," she said quietly. She shifted uncomfortably. "I do think I'll go into work for just a few hours to make sure all is well, and then be done until after the New Year."

He paused as he glanced at her. "You okay? You don't sound convinced."

"Oh no, totally good." She hated lying to Josh. But she wasn't ready to tell him why she was being cagey.

Her test was this morning and she wanted to go it alone. Until she knew something, there was just simply nothing to tell him.

At least, that's what she was going to tell herself. And today, of all days, was not the day to bring the mood down a notch.

"I'm so excited for tonight," she said earnestly.

"Me, too." He finished getting dressed and walked over to her, sitting down next to her on the edge of the bed. He leaned over and gave her a loving, gentle kiss.

"Leave around 7?"

"Perfect."

He kissed her again and then he was out the door. "Love you!"

"Love you, too," she shouted as she heard his footsteps disappear down the hallway to his office.

She really did love him. And she really hoped she could give him everything he wanted. She touched her stomach.

She hoped she could give herself everything she wanted, too.

Josh straightened his rich, navy-blue tie and silver tie pin as he waited in the living room for Scout.

"What do you think, Buster?"
Josh asked. The golden retriever
wagged his tail, then yawned as he
laid back down. "That does not
inspire confidence, buddy."

He laughed as Scout said, "I like
your tie."

The breath caught in his throat
as he peered at the woman he was
about to ask to be his wife. She was
dressed in a body-hugging,
strapless, red sheath dress. The top
was like a corset, putting her
heaving breasts on beautiful
display, and cinching her waist in a
way that illuminated her curves.
Her bright green eyes were filled
with love and those burgundy lips
were perfect and full.

He couldn't believe he got to have this woman for the rest of his life. "You're beautiful."

"Thank you." She sauntered up to him and slid her hands up his chest as he wrapped his hands around her waist, then kissed her deeply.

"Mmm," he murmured.

"Yeah," she whispered.

"Come here." He could feel his nerves start to flare. This was it. He'd thought long and hard about where to ask Scout to marry him, and always he ended up at the Christmas tree in their living room.

On it was an ornament that she had bought him that first day a year ago when he took her out for lunch, and they walked around San Diego with all its decorations. It was a

bright red heart that simply read,
"Our First Christmas," and she'd
had their names written on the back
of it. It had been her promise, of
sorts, of things to come. This ring
was his promise back to her.

"What?" she asked.

He took her hand and led her to
the tree. It was aglow with
twinkling white lights and gold and
silver decorations. The red heart
was the only red ornament, so it
stood out. Scout had done that on
purpose.

"Remember when you bought
me this?"

She grinned and nodded. "I
knew we had something special. I
wanted to commemorate it."

"Yeah." He kissed her gently and his heart ticked up a notch. He pulled back and smiled.

"What?" she asked.

He dropped down to one knee and pulled the ring box out of his jacket pocket. "Scout."

"Oh my God," she exclaimed. She put her hands to her face. "Josh."

He could see the genuine joy on her face as he opened the ring box.

"Scout, I knew then and I know now, you're the perfect woman for me."

He took the ring from the box and held her left hand in his.

"I want every Christmas to be with you. I want to spend the rest of my life with you. Raise a family with you."

At the mention of family, Josh
saw a fleeting look of…something,
in her eyes. What it was, he
couldn't be sure, but he didn't think
it was going to stop her from
saying yes.

"Will you marry me?"

There was a slight pause as she
smiled at him, and he suddenly felt
something in his gut. Something
was off. Something that meant she
might not say yes.

"Scout?"

"Josh," she whispered.

He felt a sinking, sick feeling in
his stomach as her eyes churned
with something he couldn't quite
put his finger on.

"Josh, yes, I want to spend my
life with you, of course," she said.

He felt a wave of relief wash over him as he exhaled. "Oh my God, you scared me there for a second."

"I'm sorry, I know, I, I shouldn't have paused like that," she said. She half-laughed. "Spending forever with you is what I want. I just…"

He felt that sick feeling again. "You just what?"

"I don't know if I want to be married."

Josh could feel all the air leave his lungs as he peered into her green eyes and saw uncertainty.

**6**

## Tradition

Scout knew Josh had been thinking about forever—they had communicated as much to each other over the last few months. And she had been thinking about what she would say if he asked the question: Will you marry me?

And the words "I don't know" were not part of any of the scenarios that had run through her head. Most of them were her saying yes because it was Josh and she loved him and there wasn't anyone else and never could be.

There were a couple that were more like, "Yes, but…," like commitment instead of marriage, but it was always some form of yes.

Never, in anything she had imagined, did she ever say any variation of "I don't know."

"What?" He shook his head in confusion. "But I thought—"

"You thought right," she interrupted. She felt her heart contract with guilt as she took in his carefully pressed suit, his shaved face, the beautiful ring. "I want you, Josh. I want to be with you. I definitely want that ring on my finger. It's just…"

She looked in his eyes and saw the love mixed with confusion emanating from them.

"Just what?" he asked.

"Is there a different way to do it? Like, a commitment ceremony instead of marriage?"

He glanced at the floor and back to her. It was crushing to know she was causing that pained look on his face. She was ruining their anniversary. His proposal.

"Josh, I—"

"Scout, I get it. I know you're agreeing to forever with me. I'm just…I'm a little caught off-guard."

"I know, I'm sorry." She wanted to touch him, to kiss him, to connect with him, but she could tell he was still processing the information. Best to give him a little space.

He took a deep breath and finally settled his eyes on her.

"Scout, do you want to wear this ring and be committed?" he asked.

She smiled broadly. "More than anything, Josh."

He grinned and she felt some of the air return to the room.

"Okay, I'll take that for now," he said.

He slid the ring on her finger and stood up as they each took a moment to regard its beauty. It was stunning, with one ample diamond in the center and surrounded by smaller diamonds on either side. The cluster was set on a thick, platinum band.

"It's so beautiful, Josh," she said quietly. "I love it."

"It was my grandma's. The center stone." He ran his finger over it and then gazed in her eyes. "I think we have something as special as they did."

"We do," she agreed.

"Then why?"

She took a deep breath and
exhaled slowly. They needed to
have this conversation. She needed
him to know how much she loved
him and wanted to be with him.

"We never really talked about
this, did we?" she asked.

He shook his head. "I guess we
didn't. I just…I assumed."

"Well, you weren't wrong," she
said. "We both want forever."

"You don't want marriage at
all?"

She paused as she stepped into
him. He slid his hands around her
waist.

"I want to give you what you
want, Josh," she said. She searched
his eyes for understanding. "I also
want to be true to who I am. And I
just don't think I've decided on

where I stand yet. All I know is there is no one else for me. I want to be committed to you. I'm saying yes to that."

He nodded. "Okay, I'm glad for that. I feel the same way."

"Okay," she said quietly.

He took a deep breath then sighed. "But, Scout, I want to be married. I don't want to pressure you, I know it sounds like that, but it's not. It's just, marriage is what I want. With you."

"I understand that, Josh, but I'm just not sure."

"What about kids?"

"What about them?" she asked defensively. It was too defensive, and she could see that on his face. She was stressed about the test. The doctor said it might be a day or two before she got the results, and she was on edge about the whole thing.

What if she did have endometriosis and couldn't give him children? Would he even want to marry her?

"I don't want to have children without being married, Scout."

"What does that mean?" she asked. She saw the confusion in his eyes that likely echoed her own. "You won't be with me if I don't marry you?"

"That's not…" He ran his hands through his hair and sighed. "I didn't say that."

A heavy silence fell between them.

"This isn't what I expected for tonight," he said. He sighed.

She nodded. "Let's just…can we just have a nice anniversary dinner and celebrate our commitment to each other? And have this conversation tomorrow?"

He cleared his throat and straightened his tie. He mustered a smile as he looked at her. "Yeah. I can do that."

"Okay."

He turned away from her and walked toward the garage.

"Josh?"

He turned back to her. "We'll talk tomorrow, yeah?"

She nodded.

He held out his hand and she walked to him. He took her hand in his and kissed it, then led her out to the garage.

She wasn't convinced he'd be okay with just a commitment and not marriage. She also wasn't convinced that it wouldn't kill her if he walked away.

Josh was everything to her. But she had grown up understanding that relationships were about two complete individuals coming together and having a life. If she just said yes and it was only about what Josh wanted—that was a recipe for disaster.

She just needed some time to think it through. She needed to get her test results. And then, she'd be able to give him her answer.

The only question was, would he be patient and wait?

7

## Little Red Slip

Scout waking up alone in their bed was a reminder of the way their anniversary night had ended. Dinner had been nice enough with the restaurant's signature Miso Glazed Sea Bass and wine, but Josh could only hold back his disappointment for so long. By the time they'd gotten home, there was only silence left between them, and then a gap of space in their bed.

"Josh?"

The house was silent. No Josh. No Buster. No nothing. She glanced at the clock. 8 a.m. Time for Buster's walk. They were probably already down the street and on their way back by now.

She glanced down at her ring. It was stunning and she was so proud to wear it. She touched her stomach then checked her phone. Nothing from the doctor, either.

"I'll cook something special," she whispered. She hauled herself out of their comfy bed and glanced at herself in the mirror. She was wearing a short, red lacy nightie. "So much for that."

Sex had been the last thing on Josh's mind as he grappled with her yes and her "not sure." Her advances fell short and led to more space between them. Now it was morning, and the distance was obvious.

She quickly used the restroom, washed her hands, and headed to the kitchen.

She had a roast in the fridge and potatoes and carrots. It was one of Josh's favorite meals. Maybe that would get him talking? She pulled the beef and vegetables out and placed them on the counter, then grabbed a paring knife and the spices.

"Crock pot." Shit. Crock pot was in the basement. She softly padded to the basement door and headed downstairs. Their basement was super cozy with hardwood floors, comfortable rugs, plush furniture, a small bar, a dart board, pool table and big screen. On the other side of the wall, where she was headed, was a storage space with shelves and containers. It was unfinished, but Josh had cleaned it and made it nice for stowing things away.

She twitched her nose as she scanned the shelves that had all the extra cookware. Of course, the crock pot was at the top because Josh had put it away. She turned to grab the step stool just as Josh walked in.

"Josh!" She jumped at the sight of him.

"Sorry," he said. "I saw the door was open, so I came to check on you."

"Oh, thank you," she said. She gave him a light smile and got a polite nod back. "Josh. We have to talk about this."

"I'm just not—"

They both looked at each other as the basement door slammed shut.

"Buster," Josh said.

"Josh," Scout said with a warning tone. "You didn't lock the door by accident again, did you?"

"Oh shit." Josh raced up the stairs. "Fuck!"

She could hear the loud bang of his foot against the door as she shook her head. Hey, if they were going to be trapped, their basement wasn't a bad place for it. Unfortunately, being trapped in their basement during a heated argument was not ideal.

She tried smiling at him again when he reappeared.

"Do you have your phone?" he asked.

She shook her head.

"Great."

"Yours is?"

"On the kitchen counter by the roast."

"Ah," she said quietly. "I was making you dinner."

"Thank you."

He looked her over. "Were you wearing that last night?"

She glanced down at the sexy number then back at him. "Yep."

"Huh."

"You didn't notice?"

"I was mad, Scout," he said tersely. "And hurt. And confused."

"Josh, I know you're all of those things, but we can't do anything about it unless we talk."

"I can't talk when you look like that," he said. She saw his expression soften.

"Oh," she said. Yes. This is what they needed. Sex. Sex wouldn't fix it, she knew that, but it would definitely open the door for connection. And connection would lead to talking.

She did her best stripper walk up to him and dropped one silky red strap off her shoulder. "Is this distracting you?"

"Stop it," he said huskily. She could see he was already firm just watching her.

"Stop what?" she asked silkily. She dropped the other strap off her shoulder as her nightie tumbled down her body and delicately fainted onto the floor.

"Scout." His breath caught as she stood naked before him.

"Yes, baby?"

He stripped off his gym clothes, then pulled her into a deep kiss. "I want you, baby."

"I want you, too," she panted. She was already wet for him when he slid his fingers inside her and ran his thumb over her sensitive spot. "Josh."

Her legs were trembling from the pleasure as he rubbed that spot again and again.

"I need you, Scout."

"Take me."

Josh picked her up and carried her to the plush sofa in the game room. He laid her down, then positioned himself between her legs and kissed her deeply.

"Baby, yes," she moaned.

As he entered her, all she could think was that she wanted the rest

of her life to be just like this, and
only with him.

# 8

## The Same Page

As Josh lay on the soft, cream-leather couch with Scout in his arms, he knew this is what he wanted. And whether it was legal really didn't matter. He knew that in his brain. He was having a much harder time making sense of it in his heart.

"Josh?"

He looked into her eyes and saw the love there, the absolute devotion. She was his. There was simply no question about it.

"I love you, Scout."

"I love you, too."

He ran his finger up and down her bare back as they lay together warm and cozy.

"I know we're committed to each other, Scout," he said. He adjusted his head against the soft, fuzzy pillow. "I just…I always had this picture in my mind."

"I know," she said quietly.

"Haven't you ever thought about it?" he asked. He lifted her face to look at him. "Not just generally, but with me?"

"I have," she said.

"And?"

"And it was perfect," she said. She shrugged her toned shoulders as her long hair tumbled down her back. "Absolutely perfect."

"Then what?"

"I'm not sure," she said. She played with the hair on his chest as she let out a sigh. "You know how my mom is. You met her."

"But that's your mom, Scout, that's not you," he said. He glanced up when Buster started whining at the basement door, then back to her. "You're different people. And I hate to point out the obvious, but your mom is married to your dad."

Scout laughed and when she did, he couldn't help but follow suit. Her warmth came through the baritone notes of her voice.

"That's so true," she admitted. "But my mom was from a different time. It was expected of her. And I think that's her point. I think."

"What? That it shouldn't be expected?"

She nodded. "I feel like she wants me to feel like I *want* to be married and not that I *have* to be married. Or am expected to. And something about that makes sense to me, Josh."

She touched his chin and pulled his face closer. "I love you so much. I think I need to feel like this is a decision we make together. That we're both comfortable with. I feel like marriage is a decision. You know? Being together forever...that's a given, Josh. A no-brainer. But being married? That's a choice. A big, heavy one. And I want to feel like we're making it together and that I'm not just being swept into it."

"Okay," he said tentatively. He wasn't sure he was on the same page with her, but he was starting to feel like he was getting there. And what if he had a daughter someday and what if she wanted something different than was expected? He wouldn't want to be an asshole. He'd want to support her. So, he needed to do that now for Scout. "I think I get it. One is emotional, one is practical…kind of?"

She sat up then and gazed down at him. Fuck, it was hard to concentrate when her breasts were on display like that, her green eyes peering down at him. She grinned.

"I know what you're thinking," she said with a sultry tone. "Stop that."

He laughed. "Well, put a shirt on, you little vixen. You know I can't concentrate when you're sexy like that."

He reached for her breasts, and she playfully slapped his hand away before grabbing a pillow and covering her chest.

"Dammit, that's even sexier, baby," he said.

"You can have seconds later, baby."

"Fine," he pouted.

She leaned against the couch and looked down at him as he adjusted himself to look directly up at her.

"Yes, that's kind of it," she said. "Being in love with you? Easy. It takes nothing except you and me for there to be passion and love."

"Damn straight," he whispered as he trailed a finger down her bare leg.

"Marriage is something else entirely," she said. "It's, legit, a contract. It's bills and houses and kids and schools and where are we going to live? And what does our life look like? And how do we join our money or not join our money? Who works? Who pays for what? I mean, Josh, we haven't *really* talked about those things. I think we've both just made some assumptions. I mean, do you think we've had that conversation?"

"I guess I didn't think we had to," he said. He shrugged. "I really just thought, yeah, I mean I assumed we were thinking the same thing."

She nodded as a weighty silence fell between them.

"Scout, would you want to move back to Pittsburgh? Double Digits? The whole thing."

She took a deep breath and exhaled it slowly. It made him

nervous. He wasn't sure if she was thinking of how to tell him no or if she was just simply thinking.

"I love my job here," she said quietly. "I really love California, too."

"I know." He took a deep breath. He already knew she felt like that. His heart dropped a little.

"But," she said. He perked up and smiled at her. It was good to see she was smiling back. Maybe there was hope? "You know how much I cared for Paps and for Double Digits. I'd be lying if I said that the thought of going back wasn't tempting. Plus, I'm an only child. And having Lucas, and now Jaime. Yeah. It's definitely something to think about. Maybe in a few years."

He tried to hide his
disappointment at her timeline
because the real win was that she
was open to it. Which meant he'd
have to tell Lucas not yet. And that
broke his heart a little bit, too.
Their lives were changing, and he
wanted to be there. He wanted to be
a bigger part of his brother's life,
especially now that Lucas was
having a baby of his own.

Josh was torn and he wasn't sure
how to reconcile it. He wanted to
push a little more on this
conversation, but he felt like he
didn't want to rock the boat. Not
right now.

"Okay," he said. He lightly
touched her face and she leaned
into his hand. It made his heart
leap.

"What the hell?" he exclaimed as they both jumped at the slamming door upstairs and Buster barking his head off.

"Oh, thank God," Scout said. She jumped off the couch and dropped the pillow to the floor. "Your brother."

"We're down here!" She yelled at the ceiling. She ran into the storage area, grabbed their clothes, and ran back out, dropping them all on the couch as she started putting on her slip.

Josh jumped up and got dressed, too, just as the basement door opened and Lucas hollered down, "Your basement door was locked."

"No shit," Josh yelled.

"Oh, okay asshole," Lucas said. He laughed and shut the door again.

"Think he locked it again?" Josh asked.

"Odds are," Scout replied as she laughed.

"We can always just stay down here and get back to our extracurricular activity," he said as he tried to pull her in.

"I have dinner to make," she said. "And I need the crock pot."

"Yeah, I'll get the crock pot." He pointed at her. "And you grab something from the winter clothes bin to put over that little red number you're wearing."

She looked down at her skimpy lingerie. "Oh. Right."

"Yeah," he said with a laugh. As
she moved to get something to
throw over her slip of a nightie, he
grabbed a small key from a drawer
in the side table.

Scout was right, he knew that.
There was more to talk about.

He wanted to marry her. He
knew she wasn't sure. So, what he
needed to understand, before
anything else, was what would
make her comfortable enough to
say yes—to him, to Double Digits,
and to Pittsburgh?

# 9

## Baby Dreaming

Scout could feel Jaime eyeing her as she sliced the russet potatoes and chopped the unpeeled carrots. She dropped them into the crock pot filled with the seared roast and French Onion soup.

"What?" Scout asked.

"What?" Jaime asked back. She feigned confusion as she leaned against the fridge.

"You seem like you want to ask me something," Scout said. She plopped another cut potato into the French onion broth.

"I just, I love your ring," Jaime said. She grabbed Scout's hand before Scout could get hold of another potato. "It's really…wow."

"Thank you," Scout said politely. She pulled her hand back and grabbed a potato, peeling it, then cutting it and dropping it into the broth. "And your question is?"

Scout leaned on the counter and gave Jaime an eyebrow raise.

"Oh, fine, how could you say no?" Jaime exclaimed. She stood straight and flailed her hands.

"Oh my God, I didn't say no," Scout said defensively as she waved her knife.

"You didn't say yes," Jaime countered.

"I did say yes," Scout said frustrated. "I said yes to forever. I just…Josh and I have things we need to talk about."

"Like?" Jaime pressed.

"Stuff," Scout said trying to avoid Jaime's persistent stare.

"Such as? Come on, the boys are golfing, they'll be gone for hours."

Scout sighed as she looked into Jaime's curious eyes. She wasn't going to be able to get out of this conversation. And honestly, she didn't want to. She hadn't told anyone about her test, and she was still anxiously awaiting the results. She needed to confide in someone. And why not Jaime? Who was basically her sister-in-law for all intents and purposes.

"Fine," Scout sighed as she dropped the knife on the counter.

"I knew there was something," Jaime said excitedly as she rubbed her baby belly. "Spill."

Scout took a deep breath and put the lid on the crock pot. She turned it on and moved to stand right across from Jaime.

"I'm waiting on test results," Scout said quietly.

"Test results?" Jaime's look went from curious to concern. "Scout. For what?"

"Endometriosis." Scout's eyes immediately filled with tears. She hadn't expected them—didn't realize how much stress it was causing her until she said it out loud. When she felt Jaime's arms around her, she cried for the first time since the doctor had told her of the possibility.

"Oh, Scout," Jaime said. "I'm sorry. When are you supposed to find out?"

Scout shrugged as she pulled
back and wiped her eyes. She
yanked a tissue out of the box on
the counter. "Today or tomorrow,
probably."

Jaime nodded as her delicate
hands rubbed Scout's shoulders.
The comfort was welcome.

"You're worried about fertility
issues?"

Scout nodded. "I haven't told
Josh yet because maybe there's
nothing to worry about, you
know?"

"But, Scout, this is why you
have relationships. Marriage."

Scout threw the tissue away and
looked into Jaime's caring eyes.

"The relationship is what you
lean on while you're going through

the uncertainty," Jaime said. "Not having all the answers is part of it."

"I hadn't really thought of it like that," Scout said. She wiped her eyes to clear out the bleeding mascara from her tears.

"Doesn't surprise me," Jaime quipped. She grinned. "You and Josh are both like that. Like, you have to have all the answers before you talk about it. But the whole point of talking is to get to the answer."

"You're very wise," Scout joked.

Jaime laughed. "You learn a lot from being married twice."

"I don't know how to tell him, Jaime," Scout said. Her eyes started watering again. "He wants kids so badly. And so do I."

"Knowing Josh, I feel like, it'll hurt, but it won't make a difference in his commitment to you and your life together," Jaime said. "If there is a problem, there are so many options that exist today. The least of which is better treatment for endometriosis. And then, other options like adoption or IVF or surrogacy."

Scout nodded. "I just." She let out a heavy sigh. "I just wanted to carry my own, you know? Josh's."

"I know," Jaime said quietly. She rubbed Scout's arm. "Is that why you're iffy on marriage?"

Scout shook her head. "No," she said. "I mean, yes. Because, when I think about all the things Josh and I need to figure out, children are one of them. And I don't feel like I can

say yes until I know, and he knows,
and we've talked."

Jaime nodded. "I get that."

"But, really, it's about not
wanting to feel forced into it. I
want to feel like I was part of
making the decision to be married.
I'm a planner, you know? I like to
talk through it. I like to be invested
in it. In big decisions."

"Now that, I do get," she said.
She grinned. "The level you're at in
your career. Independent. I can see
that from you. The idea of it being
a big, huge decision, and wanting
to hash it before you commit. I get
it."

"That's what Josh said. That he
'got' it."

She gave a weary smile to Jaime as she crossed her arms and rubbed them.

"You don't think he does?" Jaime asked.

"I think he wants to," Scout said. "I think, though, he has these plans and ideas in his head, and I don't know what they are or if I'm on board, too."

"Ah, so that's the thing, then." Jaime nodded her head. "You two aren't on the same page yet."

Scout nodded.

"Notice, though, I said *yet*," Jaime said softly. "You need to tell him, test results or no."

Scout nodded. "I know."

"Okay," Jaime said. "Now, can I help with anything?"

"You mean now that everything's peeled and in the crock pot and there's nothing left to do?" Scout gave her a side glance.

"That's exactly what I meant," Jaime said. She laughed and Scout couldn't help but laugh with her. "I'm pregnant. I'm here to eat."

"You can't use that excuse forever," Scout warned as she grabbed a bottle of water from the fridge and cracked it open.

"You're right," Jaime said. "So, I'm making good use of it now and for the next five months. You wouldn't believe the things I make Lucas do for me under the guise of pregnancy."

Scout laughed. "Lucas deserves it."

"Yes, he does," Jaime said with a wink. "Now, where's lunch?"

"We're ordering out." Scout took a swig of her cold water. It felt good against her throat after getting so emotional.

"Thank God," Jaime said as she walked away. "Okay. I have to pee. Again. Be right back."

Scout smiled as Jaime walked away, then picked up her phone to order lunch. As she did, she saw the doctor's number on her phone.

"Oh no," Scout whispered. She walked out of the kitchen and into the privacy of Josh's office as she took the call and prayed everything would be okay.

**10**

**Pittsburgh Scheming**

Josh shanked his golf ball into a sand pit off the ninth hole of the Torrey Pines Golf Course as Lucas laughed.

"Dude." He shook his head. "Your game is way off today."

"Yeah well," Josh said. He shoved his club into his bag and jumped on the golf cart as Lucas hopped into the driver's seat and took off.

"Look, she said no—"

"She didn't say no," Josh interrupted. Now he was annoyed. They hadn't told anyone what happened except Lucas and Jaime and that was enough for now. If they told anyone, it would bring up the question of when the wedding was and Josh was supposed to say…what? What would he say?

"She loves you, Josh," Lucas said as he navigated the cart up and down the soft hills of the course that had stunning views of the Pacific Ocean. "She just wants a conversation. I mean, you haven't even told her about the job offer. So, in a way, she's right."

"Okay, you've been married all of what, six, seven months? You don't know."

"I know more than you," Lucas said. "I am married."

Josh gave his smiling brother a look that could kill.

"Did you and Jaime have this problem?"

"Nope," Lucas said. He shrugged as sweat dripped down his forehead. He wiped it off with the back of his free hand. "But Jaime isn't Scout."

Josh shrugged as they crested a hill and the clubhouse came into full view. It was a gorgeous facility with a pool full of people and three tennis courts in action.

"Look, I don't wanna be an asshole, here, but I've got a wife— a partner—on me about this stuff, too," Lucas said. He glanced at Josh as he abruptly stopped the cart. "Our family, we need more balance. And as the current CEO, there isn't anyone besides Scout I would transition this role to. And not because she's family, because she's good. The headhunter I used said as much."

"If you used a headhunter then you have a short list," Josh said tightly.

"I don't want the short list, I want the number one and that is Scout, Josh," Lucas pressed. "So…either you tell her directly what I've offered, or I will."

Josh let out a deep sigh and grimaced at his brother. "So that's why you're here. To recruit Scout."

"It's the main reason," Lucas said. "It's our family business, man. You know Paps would want this. He was already eyeing Scout before he died. This shouldn't be news to you. Or her."

Josh nodded.

"And it's not just about recruiting Scout," Lucas said. "I meant it when I said I missed having you around. I do, man. I want you back in Pittsburgh. Shoot me."

Josh couldn't help the laugh that escaped his chest. He pulled at his shirt to give a little relief to the heat building from their rounds of golf.

"Oh, only if I could."

They both laughed as Josh finally nodded at Lucas to acknowledge what he'd said.

"What if she says no?" Josh asked.

"She won't say no."

"No, I mean, what if she says *no*?" Josh looked at Lucas. "What if I tell her what I really want, and she says no?"

"What if you lie to her to get her to marry you and five years down the road she still says no? But now it's been five years and you've wasted your time?"

Josh gave his brother a side glance. "When the hell did you get so damn smart?"

Lucas laughed. "I've always been this smart," he said. "Too bad I'm also so damn good lookin'. Really put a damper on your game all those years."

"Give me a break." Josh shook his head as Lucas started the cart up and they headed for the club.

"Don't be jealous," Lucas said with a laugh.

Josh shook his head as he enjoyed the warm wind on his face. He knew Lucas was right. He'd

have to tell Scout the truth about
what he really wanted and let the
chips fall where they may.

# 11

## We've Got a Plan

Lucas breezed into the light blue guest room of Josh and Scout's home and found Jaime anxiously waiting for him. She was pacing the hardwood floor as he walked in.

"Oh my God!" she exclaimed. She rushed behind him after he crossed into the room. "What took you so long? I'm dying here!"

She quickly but quietly shut the door and turned to face him.

"What? What's going on?" Her eyes were lit up and her hands were already moving with excitement. He knew this look—she had gossip. And not just the day-to-day mom gossip from the daycare he was used to—this was juicy gossip.

"You have to tell me right now,
Jaime, you know how much I love
when you know stuff."

"I can't tell you," she quipped.

"What the actual hell, Jaime?"
He raised his voice, and she
quickly shushed him.

"Lucas, shush!" She gave him a
light slap on the arm.

"Fine," he hissed. They eyed
each other for a second. "I've got
news, too."

"What?" she exclaimed. She
slapped his arm again.

"Shhhhhh," he hissed.

"What?" she whispered as she
hunched down.

He laughed at his adorable wife.
She was the brightest light he'd
ever had in his world. "You're
cute."

They grinned at each other for a second.

"You don't know anything," she said annoyed as she stepped back and rubbed her belly. She walked away toward the window.

"I do, too," he said defensively as he followed. "I know stuff."

She turned around and eyed him. He eyed her back.

"Pfft, you don't anything, either," he said. He tossed his ball cap on the dresser and jumped on the bed.

"Yes, I do!" she exclaimed.

He immediately jumped off the bed and stood in front of her.

"Okay, what do you know?" he asked excitedly. Jaime had such an exciting way about her. She was always fun, and she always kept up with him, no matter the scheme, the dream, or the consequences. She knew how to play, and after being a competitive athlete, she was good at games.

He narrowed his eyes at her as he raised a devilish eyebrow.

"Okay, maybe you do know something," she countered. "Well, what is it?"

They stared each other down before she finally sighed.

"Okay, on three," she relented. He nodded. "One, two—"

"Scout is worried she can't have children and hasn't told Josh."

"Josh hasn't told Scout about the job or moving to Pittsburgh."

"Josh hasn't told her yet?" Jaime exclaimed.

"Scout hasn't told Josh she can't have kids?"

"Honey, that's not what I said," Jaime corrected. "I said she's *worried* she can't have kids. She's waiting on test results about endometriosis."

"Oh," he said. "Josh floated the idea of Pittsburgh to her, but he didn't tell her why he was asking."

"Whoa," Jaime said. She flicked her hands in the air. "She doesn't know about your offer?

"Nope," Lucas said. He sat down on the edge of the bed. "Wow. Who would have guessed I'd be the mature one in this situation?"

"Uh," Jaime said hesitantly.

"Stop it," he smirked.

"Honey, what are we gonna do?" she asked. She walked over and put her hands on his shoulders and rubbed them.

"What are we, Lucy and Ricky Ricardo running schemes?" He grabbed her hips and gave them a playful squeeze. "This isn't *I Love Lucy*. We're not gonna do anything."

"Oh, honey, we *are* Lucy and Ricky. That's our job as the younger couple."

She gripped his face in her hands and kissed him lightly before gazing into his eyes. He loved when she did that. Her eyes were like blue diamonds, and he could stare into them all day.

"We're like two years younger, babe," he said. "Basically, the same age."

"Younger is younger," she said
She shrugged as she stood straight.
"We need to do something. They're
perfect together. They're both just
really terrible at this part of the
relationship. We have to help them,
babe."

"No, babe."

"Babe. We're doing it."

"Fine." Lucas relented as he
grabbed her hips and gently pulled
her back to him then down onto his
lap. He gave her a light kiss.
"Damn, I love you. I'm so lucky."

"You really are." They both
laughed as Lucas put his hand on
her belly. Then it hit him.

"The baby," he said.

"What about her?"

"Her? Is it a her?" Lucas got excited as he stared in surprise at . his beautiful wife.

"Don't know, just trying it out."

"That's not funny."

She grinned at him.

"No, I mean, the baby needs godparents," Lucas said. "What if we asked them to be the godparents and doing that forced them to have a conversation?"

"Oh, I love the idea of them being godparents." She cupped his face and kissed him.

"Right?"

"Totally," she said. "But that's a terrible idea. What if we just lock them in the basement again and tell them we won't let them out until they fix it?"

"Josh would murder me."

They eyed each other again, each trying to read the other's thoughts as though marriage had made them suddenly capable of ESP.

"What if we 'accidentally' locked them in the basement, left and pretended we didn't realize we did it?" he asked.

"I love it," she exclaimed. Maybe they did have marriage-induced ESP? "Yes, babe."

She kissed him and ran her hands over his chest.

"Oh shit, do I get the good lovin' right now babe?" he asked as she laid him back on the bed and straddled him. Holy shit she was sexy.

"Yeah, you do, stud," she said as she laughed and pulled her shirt off.

Her breasts had always been full and gorgeous, but pregnancy certainly added a little extra. He loved her curves. All of them.

"Hell yes!" he exclaimed as he ran his hands over her body. "Damn, I love you."

He pulled her close as late afternoon set in and they made love in the warm sunlight pouring into the room.

# 12

## The Secret Place

Josh walked into the kitchen and took a deep whiff of the delicious smell of roast and vegetables cooking.

"How was golf?" Scout asked as she walked in from the living room.

"Good," Josh said. "Uneventful."

"Oh, come now," she grimaced. "Anything with Lucas in tow is always eventful."

He laughed as he pointed at the crock pot. "Smells delicious."

"Your favorite," she said. She walked up to him as he took in her loving jade-colored eyes and those beautiful curves. She was always dressed perfectly with just the right look. And her smile could knock him dead where he stood. It was hard to be mad at her. Ever.

"It is, baby, thank you," he said warmly. He reached for her, grabbing those beautiful hips, and pulling her to him. He slid his hands up her body to her neck, then lifted her face to his. He kissed her deeply, tasting her as their tongues softly danced with each other.

"Mmm," she murmured. The sound made him harden instantly. He loved this woman in so many ways and for so many things.

No matter what was happening between them, he appreciated that Scout always took care of him, truly for better or worse. She always made sure there was food, that it was what he liked, that the

house was clean, and the laundry
was done. She did it for herself,
too, and because she loved him, she
gave those things to him as well.

He took care of her, too. He'd
get her car detailed, walk the dog,
take out the trash, wash the dishes,
and make sure she was always
satisfied, in any way she needed to
be. He did those things for himself,
too, but because he loved her, he
extended everything for himself to
her.

How could he give that up just
because she, maybe, didn't want to
be married? Couldn't long-term
commitment be just as fulfilling?

"I love you," he said quietly as
he gave her one last quick peck.

"I love you, too."

He leaned his forehead against hers. He didn't want to ruin this vibe they had going. There was too much at stake. He needed to have connection with her before they launched into a conversation that may or may not end well for them both.

"Wanna hit the lake for a bit?" he asked. The cozy lake in their neighborhood was just down the street and had a little canoe they could go get lost on the water for a bit and just enjoy themselves.

"Yeah, this won't be ready for another couple hours," she said. She peered into his eyes with relief. "Let's go spend some time together."

"Good," he said. He slid his
hands down her body and grabbed
her hand. "Let's go."

"Yeah," she said.

They wrangled the dog into the
mud room, then walked out the
front door into their small yard with
palm trees and warm-weather
vegetation. He took a deep breath
of the fresh air. He missed
Pittsburgh, but he couldn't get fresh
ocean air like this in the city. It was
one of the things he loved about
California and being so close to the
ocean.

"Love that sea air," he said. He
squeezed her hand.

"Right?" she asked. She took a
deep breath. "I've loved being here
with you."

"Me, too, baby," he said. He grinned at her as she smiled and slid on her sunglasses. It was late afternoon as they turned onto the sidewalk into their neighborhood. Little kids were getting home from school and running from the bus to their houses. They were playing with each other, glad to be free from their elementary teachers for the holidays and yelling and screaming with joy.

"Remember being that young?" he joked. He glanced at her. "Scout, are you okay?"

"I have something in my eye," she said, quickly wiping at it underneath her Chanel lenses. "I'm good."

She gave him a megawatt smile
and he continued. "My brother and
I used to scream and play like that."

"I always wished I had siblings,"
she said. "But now I've got Lucas
and Jaime."

"You do," he said. He smiled at
her.

They walked quickly past the
kids and down a small walking path
shadowed by palm trees that led to
the lake. The canoe was where it
always was and he pushed it into
the rich dark water, leaving a little
bit on land so Scout could get in.
He held her hand as she sat down
and got comfortable. Then he put
one foot in the boat and pushed off
with the other, hopping in and
sitting down quickly. He grabbed
the paddle and pushed them further

out onto the lake into the sunshine. It sparkled brilliantly against the water, reflecting onto Scout, and giving her a soft glow.

"Let's go to the spot," she said quietly.

He grinned. "Okay."

The spot was a very secluded little grassy knoll they had found off the lake where they liked to make love. It was lined with soft grass and tall flowers and hidden in a patch of palm trees with huge leaves that gave the area privacy.

It was exactly what they needed. No words. Just action. Just bodies showing each other how much love existed between them.

He pulled the boat to the shore and hid it behind the tall lake grass. He jumped out and took Scout's hand as she gently stepped onto the ground and into his arms. They wasted no time taking each other's clothing off before finding the most hidden, shaded location and lying down together.

He kissed down her throat, to her breasts, bringing them into his mouth as she moaned. Her hands tangled into his hair as he kissed down her abdomen then tasted her womanhood under the blue sky. She moved her hips in time as her hands guided his head.

"Josh," she purred. "Baby."

He knew that moan. She was close. And so was he. He slid back up her body and positioned himself between her legs, teasing her entrance.

"I love you, Scout," he
whispered.

"Baby, I love you so much," she
said quietly.

Her moan in his ear was a
beautiful sound as he slid inside her
and the two of them exploded with
pleasure in their secret place.

## 13

## And Now You Know

Lucas paced in front of the large floor-to-ceiling windows that looked out on Josh and Scout's front yard.

"Babe, pacing isn't going to make them get here any faster," Jaime said lazily as she flipped through a magazine from her prone position on the couch.

"You know the plan?" he asked. He stopped and stared her down as she actively ignored him.

"Yep."

Lucas kept staring at her, ranging from intense to super intense.

"Are you trying to stare me into looking at you again?" she asked nonchalantly.

"Is it working?"

"Am I looking at you?"

"Damn it." He turned back to the window. "You know, this is just like Josh."

"What's just like Josh?"

"Avoiding hard conversations," Lucas said. He glanced at his Timex watch and peered out the window. He turned back to Jaime. "Baby, he would have tried to take over the company, even though he didn't really want it, because it's what he thought people wanted from him."

Jaime glanced at him from the couch, dropped her magazine on the table, and sat up, giving him her full attention.

"So, instead of having that tough conversation, he was just gonna ride that thing out." Lucas pushed the air with his hand like a surfer on a wave. "That's what he's doing now, too. It's why they're in this position. He's just gonna ride it out because he doesn't want to say what he wants. He doesn't wanna create conflict."

Jaime stood up as she walked to the window and stood with Lucas.

"Has he always been like that?"

"Always," Lucas said. "I mean, not with me. With me, he's competitive and we start shit. But we're brothers, and he knows I can take it. But, Paps, dad, Scout? He walks on eggshells."

Jaime touched her stomach then looked at Lucas and smiled.

"What?" he asked.

"I can feel him moving. Like butterflies."

Lucas felt warmth rush through his body. He knew his grin was wide and dopey as he kissed Jaimie, then bent down and kissed her stomach. He stood and gazed at her.

"Now it's a boy?"

"I'm trying it out," she said. She winked at him. He exhaled slowly, amazed that he got so lucky to have Jaime.

"You know," she said. "Josh should really know better. About Scout. That she can handle a hard conversation."

"Right? I mean, she's a boss. Look at her."

Jaime shook her head. "No, honey, that's not what I mean."

He glanced at her and saw a thoughtful expression cross her face as she smiled.

"What do you mean then?" he asked.

"Love, baby," she said quietly. "She loves him. That's what makes difficult conversations possible."

Fuck, he really did hit the jackpot. "How did I marry the smartest woman on earth?"

"I don't know, babe, you got lucky."

He laughed, then kissed her. "Damn straight, I did."

"Oh, honey, they're back." Jaime quickly moved away from the window, dragging him with her and then forcing them both to duck behind the couch.

"Babe, why are we hiding?" he asked.

She shrugged. "It just felt right."

"You're ridiculous." He laughed as he stood and pulled her up just as they heard Scout and Josh at the front door talking to a neighbor.

Lucas gave Jaime a wink. "Alright, stick to the plan," he said.

"Me?" she asked offended. "I'm Lucy."

"Exactly." They both plastered on fake grins as Josh opened the front door and walked in. He glanced at them and his brow furrowed.

"Why are you being weird?" Josh asked immediately.

"What?" Lucas said as Jaime needled his rib cage. "Why are *you* being weird?"

Josh shook his head as Scout walked in behind him.

"Have a good night!" she yelled to the neighbor.

Lucas noted their mussed hair and clothing. He glanced at Jaime and waggled his eyebrows. She grinned. He turned back to Josh.

"You've got a stick in your hair there, buddy." Lucas pointed at Josh.

"What?" Josh felt his head, then pulled the tiny, pretzel-sized stick from the side of his head. He tossed it in one of the living room plants then grinned at Lucas. "Oops."

"Mmmhmm," Lucas muttered.

Scout shut the front door then eyed them staring at each other. "What's happening?"

Lucas grinned at her, too. "You, uh, have some fun at the lake, there, Scout?"

She glanced between him and Josh, before smirking at Lucas. "You're the perfect little brother, Lucas. Annoying and juvenile."

"You're welcome for the fun," Lucas replied.

Scout chuckled as she glanced at her platinum and diamond Cartier watch that went perfectly with her diamond ring.

"Dinner should be ready in thirty," she said. She smiled at Jaime. "Wanna help me set the table?"

"Oh, sure, yeah," Jaime quipped. She shot a glance at Lucas who gave her knowing wink. "But, uh, wait, before you do that, I was hoping…did you say you had some winter sweaters I could take back with me to Pittsburgh?"

"Oh, yeah, they're in the basement," Scout said. She walked past Jaime toward the dining room.

"Can I grab those real quick?" Jaime asked. She started toward the basement. "Now."

"Oh, uh," Scout said as she stopped and looked questioningly at Jaime. "Sure."

Scout shrugged as she walked to the basement door, opened it, and headed down.

"Hey, wanna shoot a game of pool real quick before dinner?" Lucas asked Josh.

"What are you doing?" Josh asked suspiciously.

"Trying to kill time." Lucas shrugged in as convincing a way as possible.

"Yeah, whatever," Josh said. Lucas followed him to the basement door as Josh made his way down.

"Oh, hang on, I gotta pee, I'll be down in a sec," Lucas yelled down the stairs. Lucas quietly stepped back, shut the door, and locked it. He ran back into the dining room and did a little dance with Jaime.

"We're so damn good," Lucas said like a champion winning the Stanley Cup.

"Yeah, we are." Jaime did something like a twerk unsuccessfully and he followed suit as they both laughed.

"Now he has to tell her about the job offer back in Pittsburgh," Lucas said.

"And she has to tell him about the baby thing," Jaime said.

"What baby thing?" Josh asked.

Lucas and Jaime froze as they whipped around to see Josh's stunned face.

"But, the door, the lock," Lucas said stunned as Scout walked up beside Josh and dropped the sweaters, equally stunned.

"I put the key on the door frame inside the basement," Josh said. "What baby?"

"What offer in Pittsburgh?" Scout asked.

Lucas and Jaime couldn't speak as they stared at the other couple.

"We want you to be our baby's godparents!" Jaime exclaimed.

"Yay!" Lucas exclaimed, following suit, and throwing his hands in the air. He had to admire his wife for trying to enact some kind of distraction plan after this disaster they had created.

Scout slowly turned to look at Josh. "Josh? What offer?"

He faced her. "What baby?"

Lucas glanced to Jaime as he dropped his hands. "Nice job, Lucy."

"Oh, shut it, Ricky." She put her hands on her hips as they stared at Josh and Scout and waited for the

storm of an argument they had
created.

# 14

## From Here to There

Scout could feel the hot tears building before anything was even said. This fight had been brewing since he proposed. And now, it appeared, she wasn't the only one hiding something.

"Josh?" she implored.

"What baby, Scout?" he asked again sternly. He turned to face her and she could see a stormy sea of emotions tearing across his eyes. Everything in him was tense and tight.

This is not the way she wanted Josh to find out about her test results. In the heat of an angry moment. But here it was, so, better to get it over with quickly.

"Josh, I have endometriosis,"
Scout said. She said it quick, like
ripping off a Band-Aid, and hoped
that somehow the speed of the
delivery would lessen its impact. It
didn't.

"What?" he asked, frustrated.
His hands flailed up and then down
to his hips. Confusion spread from
his face to his whole body. He
glanced at Lucas and Jaime, then
back to her. "What?"

"The pain I've been having, the
doctor, the other day, she felt
something during my exam," she
said quietly. "There was some
hardening, maybe scar tissue. And
she sent me for tests."

She took one look at the searing
pain and anger on his face then cast

her stare aside. It wasn't until this moment she realized how painful it must be for him to know she went through this without him. Left him in the dark about something that impacted them both. Why had she thought for even a second that was okay to do? "I'm sorry."

"I asked you, Scout, I asked you directly what the doctor said, and you said there was nothing," he yelled. "And how the hell does my brother know and I don't? Scout!"

"I'm sorry, I know, I'm sorry," she said. The tears started to fall as she glanced at him. She could see it in his face how wrong she had been to keep it from him.

"And you had tests?" he asked confused. "What tests?"

"A laparoscopy," she said, wiping away the tears.

"You had an invasive test like that alone? Damn it, Scout."

Now he was really mad. He turned and walked away, running his hands through his hair, and leaning against the sink to catch his breath.

"We are so sorry," Jaime finally said. Scout cast an angry stare at her. "Scout, I'm sorry. We thought if we could get you two to talk…"

Jaime shrugged and stopped talking as she rubbed her belly. A stark reminder to Scout that she may never be able to carry a baby. Or more specifically, to carry Josh's baby. It hit her like a ton of bricks as she glanced back to him.

"I'm sorry, Josh," she whimpered. "I should have told you, not Jaime."

"Josh, this is our fault," Lucas said. "We thought we could help, we didn't...we're so sorry."

There was a long pause before Josh finally turned around and glared at Lucas, then Scout, then back to Lucas before his face softened a touch.

"It's not your fault," Josh finally said. "This is...this is. Scout and I needed to have this conversation, so. It's on us."

"We'll leave you guys alone," Lucas said. "We'll go get a hotel."

He grabbed Jaime's hand and they turned to walk out as Josh stopped them.

"No, stay." Josh nodded at his brother as Scout peered at her love, confused. "Stay."

He faced Scout. His tone was softer. "You have it, though? Endometriosis?"

She nodded.

"What does that mean, Scout? What is it?" His voice was calmer, and Scout wasn't sure if that was a good thing given he had asked Lucas to stay.

"I have to be treated. There are a few options." She tucked a hair behind her ear. "Umm, it could mean I can't get pregnant, or I could have difficulty getting pregnant."

She couldn't stop the torrent of tears that rushed from her eyes as she squeaked like a wounded animal, burying her face in her hands. She hadn't realized how painful this truly was until she had to say it out loud to Josh.

"Scout." She felt Josh's arms wrap around her and pull her to him.

"I'm sorry," he whispered into her ear as he squeezed her tightly. "It'll be okay, Scout. You'll be okay."

She nodded into his shoulder as her hot tears started to slow.

"Is this why you didn't want to say yes?" he asked.

He pulled back as she looked up into his eyes. "Part of it."

He nodded as he wiped the wetness from her face with his thumbs. "I see."

A moment passed between them before she remembered the Pittsburgh comment. "Wait."

She stepped away from Josh and shook her head. "What job offer, Josh? What was Lucas talking about?"

Josh took a step back and inhaled sharply.

"Yeah, that," he said. He crossed his arms over his chest, looked down at the floor, then back to her. "Lucas wants to take a step back from Double Digits. With the new baby and Casey."

She could tell Josh was being careful with his words. He only did that when it was something big.

"And?" she pressed. And now she was the one feeling angry.

"Lucas would like to step down into the COO role. He wants to offer you the role of CEO. And for us to move back to Pittsburgh," Josh said matter of fact. "I'd help him during your year of non-compete and then you would take over and run it. It would be yours. Your vision."

She let out a held breath of surprise mixed with outrage. "You didn't think to tell me that?"

And now she was the one incensed, yelling at him in the dining room of their beautiful home. Something they'd never really done. And that, she suddenly realized, was the actual reason she hadn't said yes to Josh. They had never been honest enough with each other to really fight, to really test their boundaries. Everything had come so easy for them.

Not anymore.

"Are you kidding me right now?" he shouted back.

"You're unbelievable, Josh," she said. She pumped her fists next to her body, squeezing them into tight balls. "That's why you brought up Pittsburgh the other day. You were checking my reaction instead of just telling me something so huge, so significant for me, for us."

And now her fists were wide open, her hands flailing in the air.

"Well, apparently I'm not the only one holding things back," he yelled. He flicked his hand at her as the words flew heatedly from his mouth.

"See, this is why I didn't say yes to you," she yelled.

And that brought their fight to a screeching halt. A long silence fell between them.

"This is why, Josh," she said quietly. They shared a pained and knowing stare. "It's not just that we haven't talked about these things. It's about the fact we didn't think we could. I don't want to start a marriage that way. Do you?"

He shook his head. "No. No, I don't."

He let out a held breath and closed his eyes. When he opened them, he put his hands on his hips, glanced at Lucas, then Scout, and said, "You know what, you're right."

"Yeah," she said. Then she really looked in his eyes and didn't like what she saw there. "Wait, what does that mean?"

She felt a sinking feeling in her gut as he let out a sigh.

"Lucas needs some help right now while they get ready for the baby so," he said. He paused as he looked at her. "I'm gonna go to Pittsburgh for the holidays. Just, let's take a little time, okay? And, after the New Year, we can talk through this."

She felt her stomach drop as her eyes started to twitch with tears. She almost said no and begged him to stay, but she held it back. He was right. And she hated that he was.

She loved Josh with all her heart, and she knew he loved her. That

had never been the issue. The issue
was they were so in love they
didn't want to test it. Didn't want to
stir the pot and say the hard things.

The fact was, they had kept
things, big things, from each other,
because they were too scared to put
their relationship to the test. It was
a jarring reality. She was a C-Suite
executive with hundreds of people
relying on her to do the hard things
so they could keep their jobs and
she could help move the company
forward—which she had done,
brilliantly. And without any
hesitation.

But with Josh, her love, she was
scared to rock the boat and upset
the vibe. And if they couldn't say
the hard things, challenge each

other, did that mean their relationship was too weak to last?

She nodded. "Okay."

She saw the tears form in his eyes. "I love you, Scout. That hasn't changed. I just…let's take some time."

She nodded as she glanced at the surprised faces of Lucas and Jaime, both rendered speechless. They'd never seen Scout and Josh fight. Which was funny, because Josh and Scout had never seen Josh and Scout fight like that, either.

She sighed as she tucked a hair behind her ear. There was simply nothing left to say in this heated moment as Josh walked away and Scout did, too.

# 15

## Full Circle

Josh couldn't deny how good it felt to walk the hallways of Double Digits and have everyone in the company walk up to him and shake his hand or hug him tightly.

He straightened his tie and smiled wide as familiar faces welcomed him back to Pittsburgh and, more importantly, the company. This place was his home—the city, the business, the people. He felt about this place the same way Scout felt about StudioX. There was an ownership, a love for it, and them.

"Feels good, right?" Lucas slapped Josh's back as he moved past Josh into Pappy's office.

*Pappy's office.*

Josh shook his head. This wasn't Pappy's office anymore. It was Lucas's.

"I see you've done absolutely nothing with the place," Josh quipped. He gently chuckled as he stepped into the C-suite and shook his head. It was like he never left. He wouldn't have been surprised to see Pappy walk out of the executive bathroom and smile at him. It brough tears to his eyes. He swallowed them back as he glanced at the black and white photo of Paps and his grandma on the desk.

"I'm glad you kept it there," Josh said quietly. He pointed to the photo.

Lucas gave a nod of acknowledgement and glanced

around the office, then back to Josh.

"I didn't have the heart to change anything," Lucas said quietly.

"I see that," Josh replied. He nodded at Pappy's desk—nope. Lucas's desk. "It's like you don't even use it."

"I don't," Lucas said. He shrugged as Josh glanced at his little brother.

"What?"

"I tried. I really did," Lucas said. He leaned against the back of the black leather couch. "But it never felt right. At first, I thought it was because of Paps, you know?"

Josh nodded as he ran his finger along the black lacquer edges. Lucas walked up beside him.

"It took me the full year to realize it was because this desk, this office, it really belongs to Scout," Lucas said. He glanced at Josh, who grinned at him with a nod. "Pappy knew it, too. That's why she was always in the mix, you know? He knew she was perfect for you. He knew she was perfect for the company. Bastard always knew better."

Josh laughed as he slid his hands in his pockets. "He really did, didn't he?"

"He did," Lucas said. Josh could feel Lucas's stare on him.

"What?" Josh asked.

"Listen, I said it before, but, seriously, Jaime and I are really—"

"Stop apologizing for it," Josh interrupted. "That fight was always coming."

"Okay." Lucas nodded.

They looked out the window into downtown Pittsburgh.

"God, I miss this place," Josh said.

"We miss you."

Josh nodded as he took a deep breath.

"You know she's the one for you, right?" Lucas asked.

"Yeah."

"Good."

"We just need a little time," Josh said quietly.

"Okay," Lucas said. "Just…don't wait too long, you know?"

"I won't." Josh glanced at his brother and let out a held breath. "Now, how can I help?"

The brothers grinned at each other as they got to work.

# 16

## Moms Know

While the California sun had been shining, Scout had been crying. For three days straight she had oscillated between aching sobs and yelling at Netflix rom coms to crying silently into her pillows and eating whole pints of ice cream in one shot.

Buster had been a good companion on day one, but by day three he was sick of her, and sitting by the window looking for Josh.

"He's not coming," she cried into her pillow as she reached for a tissue. When her hand found an empty box, she threw it across the room, drug herself out of bed, and padded to the kitchen.

She was in desperate need of wine and Chinese food. She needed something to quell the unease of being this far away from Josh. She grabbed the wine and held it under her arm as she moved to the pantry.

Scout hadn't been this far apart from Josh for this long since…who was she kidding? She and Josh had never been this far apart since they made it official. Literally or figuratively.

"Where are my Oreos?" She rummaged through the pantry shelf until she heard a banging at her front door, then a shuffling, then a scraping, and then the door opening.

"Shit," she whispered. She gripped the wine bottle harder with her arm as she used her other hand

to grab a heavy can from the
pantry. She started toward the front
door. As she passed the knife block,
she traded in the can for a butcher
knife. Her heart ticked up when she
turned the corner, and screamed at
the sight of her…mother?

"Mom!" she yelled at the aging
beauty. "You were almost the
subject of a True Crime episode."

"Oh my God, honey, calm
down!" her mother shouted as she
set down her purse and an
overnight bag.

"Calm down? Do you know how
to use a phone? Good Lord."

"Oh, sweetie, look at you." Her
mom crinkled her concerned face at
Scout's wrinkled sweatpants and
shirt.

Scout annoyingly ran her hand over them while still holding the knife. Her mom walked up and pulled a cheese puff from Scout's rumpled hair, then the knife from her hand and the wine bottle from under her arm.

"Maybe you should shower."

Scout couldn't do anything but cry as her mother first held her tight, then quickly ushered her back to her room and shoved her in the shower.

Scout peered at her mother across the kitchen table as she sipped the scalding hot tea the older woman had made her. It was Earl

Gray, her favorite, with just a little extra sugar for comfort.

"Thank you, Mom," she said, casting her eyes down. There wasn't anyone else in the world she wanted to find her in the condition she had been. Only her mother could find her like that and still love her.

Or, maybe, she hoped, Josh could, too?

"You're welcome." Her mother was beautiful with rich dark hair like Scout's, but with gray starting to thread its way through. It was in a fashionable, but sensible bun at the base of her neck and her make-up was minimal. Her eyes were a bright green, also like Scout's, and her figure was the same curvy shape.

"How did you know I'd need you?" Scout put her teacup down and smiled at her.

"Moms know," her mother said matter of fact. She glanced at Scout's ring finger, then back at Scout with an eyebrow raise.

"Josh asked me to marry him."

"Oh, Scout." Her mother looked pleased as her hand gripped her shirt over her heart. "Oh, I'm so happy for you."

"What?" Scout asked confused. "You are?"

"Of course," her mother said. "Why wouldn't I be? Josh loves you. He's your partner."

"I just," Scout said. She leaned back in her chair and looked at her mother. "I thought you didn't want me to be married? That you didn't think I should be."

"Oh, well, if it was the wrong person, maybe," she said with a shrug. "Or if I really felt you didn't want to be married, maybe."

"But your gender studies and feminism and all that—I thought you didn't think I should." Scout shook her head in bewilderment.

"Oh, honey, I'm sorry it came out that way, that wasn't my intention," the elder woman said. She shook her head. "I just never wanted you to feel forced into marriage. Or that it was your only choice—that you had to do it, for someone other than yourself. That's all."

"Oh," Scout said quietly.

"Do you want to be married?"

Scout shifted in her seat.

"I think." She paused. Things were becoming clearer in her mind. Josh was right, the space had helped, even though she cried—and ate—her way through it. And now with her mother being here, it was all helping her get to the right conclusion for what she wanted.

"Mom, I don't think I did want to get married," Scout admitted. "I love my career. I don't think I ever thought marriage and my career could ever work together. You know? And I wanted a career. I love it so much."

"I get that," her mother said with a nod. "I totally get that. My work is that important to me, too."

"Yeah," Scout said. "I never thought I'd love anything more

than that, until I met Josh. And it scared me, you know?"

Her mother nodded as she reached out her hand and grabbed Scout's hand in her own.

"And I thought, how could I be so fickle and change my mind? That now, all of a sudden, I want to be married after all those years of thinking I didn't?"

Her mother smiled as Scout talked through it.

"You know, and what if I got fickle again and decided I didn't want to be married and I hurt Josh? That would just kill me."

Scout felt the tears bubble up in the backs of her eyes as her mother squeezed her hand.

"First of all, you're allowed to change your mind," her mother

said. "It's going to happen a lot
more, you know? Both of you are
going to change as you grow older
and wiser."

"How did you and dad manage
to stay together?"

Her mother shrugged. "We
stubbornly loved each other."

She squeezed Scout's hands with
vigor and love.

"We were defiant. A team. Us
against the world. And we weren't
going to lose. That was our
common ground."

Scout smiled. "Josh and I are
like that. A team."

"That's a good start," her mother
said. "But lying to him about the
tests. Your father and I, we didn't
lie to each other. Good or bad.

Even when it was ugly, we told the truth."

Scout searched her mother's eyes for more wisdom.

"How did you know it wouldn't break you, Mom?"

"We didn't," her mother said. "But any marriage worth its salt can sustain the truth. And if it can't, better to find out sooner."

Scout took a deep breath as she held her mother's hand. "I'm glad you're here."

The two shared a knowing smile as her mother gave one last squeeze and let go.

"Me, too. How about I make you some dinner? Cut up some veggies and make soup," her mother said as she stood. "I'll use the butcher knife you were going to murder me with."

"Mom!" Scout laughed as her mother walked to the kitchen.

Her mother's light laugh filled the air as she got to work cutting vegetables. Her mother wasn't the warm and fuzzy type, and never would be, but damn if she didn't love Scout more than life itself.

Scout could only hope that if she and Josh could have children someday, she'd be as good a mother as her own. And that the love she and Josh shared would be as strong as her mother's and father's was.

## 17

### What Happens in Vegas

The dinging slot machines, and bright lights of the casino were a stark reminder of how much Josh missed California. And more specifically, Scout.

He shook his head in disbelief as he sat at the Blackjack table and watched his money go down the drain.

"I'm out," Josh said to the dealer, who nodded at him. Josh stood up from the table and turned to look for his brother and dad. A showgirl in barely any clothing sauntered up to him with a grin.

"High rollers get special treatment in Vegas," she said with a grin.

"Not this high roller," Josh said with a smile. "But thanks."

"Let me know if you change your mind," she said sexily as she walked away. He enjoyed the view. He wasn't dead after all, but he certainly wasn't looking, either. He knew better—another woman wasn't going to fix his aching heart. Only Scout could do that.

"How you doing, man?" Lucas said as he walked up from behind and slapped Josh on the back.

"No way Jaime let you come to Vegas without a good reason," Josh said. He raised a suspicious eyebrow at the youngest of the traveling trio.

Lucas laughed as R.J. walked up.

"My God, do you see these beauties?" R.J. danced with one of the sexily clad beauties who walked by. "I'm convinced this is what heaven looks like."

"Too bad you won't get to see it," Josh quipped.

"Ahahahaha," Lucas laughed as R.J. smirked.

"Don't be a downer, Josh." R.J. said. "It's unbecoming."

Josh shook his head.

"No way either of you bring me to Vegas without a plan. So, what? Are you trying to get me to move on or something?"

"Hell no," R.J. said. "Never. Lucas likes her."

"And you?" Josh asked. He shoved his hands in his pants pockets.

R.J. shrugged as he looked around. "Yeah, she's grown on me. She's got a way, you know?"

"I do," Josh said.

"I'm not too keen on the fact she turned you down—"

"She did *not* turn me down," Josh said sternly.

"Tomato, tomahtoe," R.J. said with a shrug.

Lucas interrupted with a slap to Josh's arm.

"We just wanted to take your mind off everything for a quick couple days, that's all," Lucas said.

Josh gave him a hairy eyeball.

"Okay, alright, and maybe give you a little glimpse into your world without Scout," Lucas added.

"There it is," Josh said. He adjusted his shoulders as he glanced around.

"Josh, you can't run from her," R.J. said as he took a sip from the whiskey glass in his hand.

"And you can't keep hiding out in Pittsburgh, man," Lucas added.

"So, you brought me here to force my hand because you knew I'd hate it?"

"More or less." R.J. shrugged.

"Did Jaime have anything to do with this?" Josh asked.

Lucas avoided Josh's stare. "No."

"Lucas."

"Yes." He looked at Josh with a guilty grimace.

"Jaime is terrible at these schemes. Stop letting her do them."

Lucas laughed. "I can't man, I love her. And they seem stupid, but they do work."

"All evidence to the contrary."

"Josh, go home," R.J. said.

"I can't," Josh said.

"Why not?" Lucas asked. "Because if you don't, Jaime's gonna kill me."

"Look, I'm gonna bottom-line this for you two," Josh said as he brought his hands out of his pockets and animated his story with them.

"By all means," R.J. said.

"I want to marry Scout. I want to move to Pittsburgh. I want to have kids, whether that means adoption or something else. I love her," Josh said. "Or, I'd even stay in California and have no kids, if

that's what she wanted. But Scout
has to know on her own what she
wants. And I'm not going to badger
her into figuring it out. She needs
time and space to think. Whether
she knows that or not. And when
she's ready, I'll be waiting to have
that important conversation. To find
the compromise that makes us both
happy."

Lucas and R.J. nodded as they
let out a collective sigh.

"What if she goes her own way?
Without you?" Lucas asked.

Josh shook his head. "That's a
risk I have to take. We both have to
want this. And I'd rather know now
than five years from now, right? I
think someone pretty smart told me
that."

Josh grinned at Lucas who returned with a nod.

"Pretty smart? Damn brilliant I'd say," Lucas retorted.

"Good grief." Josh turned toward the exit. "Can we leave now, please?"

"Wait, one more round," R.J. said as he started to follow one of the showgirls.

"No, Dad, now," Lucas said. "Let's go."

Lucas grabbed R.J. and drug him out of the casino as Josh laughed.

Whatever he and Scout were going to be, they each needed to come into the relationship ready to talk honestly about they wanted.

That had always been hard for Josh, but he didn't want it to be hard anymore. He wanted to be

with Scout, and he knew the only
way to do that was to get real with
her, and her with him.

And he hoped, together, by
doing that, they could find the right
path forward for them both.

**18**

**The Girls Club**

Scout had no intention of spending Christmas Eve alone. She'd gotten up well before dawn, showered, dressed, and put herself together. It was a huge step up from two days ago when her mother had arrived and then subsequently left the following day with a promise from Scout to come home for Christmas.

So, Scout had packed, gotten a neighbor to watch the dog, and bought her plane tickets. The flight left in a few hours, and she'd arrive on the east coast at her parent's house sometime in the early afternoon, just in time for Christmas Eve dinner.

She glanced at Buster with his head on his paws like he knew she was leaving. His long eyelashes framed sad eyes.

"I miss him, too, buddy," she said quietly as she petted him behind his ears.

She was much closer now to making her decision about Josh and knew she was on the right path. Josh had said after the New Year they'd come back together, and she felt ready for that.

Scout had taken the time to make peace with her diagnosis and the possibility she may not be able to have children. But whether Josh would be okay with that was another story. And making peace with it didn't mean her heart wasn't broken at the thought of not having his babies.

She also now knew she wanted to commit to Josh, and hoped he still wanted that, too.

"What the?" Her Ring app went off and she glanced down at her phone to see saw none other than Katherine at her door. "Oh my goodness!"

She and Buster ran to the front of the house and Scout flung open the door as the dog ran out excitedly, barking and jumping. "Katherine!"

"Scout!" Katherine exclaimed. They gripped each other in a hug as Scout pulled her inside.

"Get in here, Buster." She waved the dog in as she shut the door and turned to the older woman in big, oversized Versace sunglasses, a smart legging and boot, and light jacket. Katherine dropped her bag to the floor, and they hugged once more.

"What are you doing here? It's Christmas Eve," Scout exclaimed.

"I know it's Christmas Eve," Katherine said as she pulled her glamorous glasses off. "I'm here to get you and bring you home where you belong."

"What?" Scout asked confused as Buster finally got bored and laid down. "No, Josh said —"

"I don't care what Josh said," Katherine quipped. She lightly touched Scout's arm. "He misses you. And I know you miss him. And it's Christmas. And you're wearing a beautiful ring given to

you in love. Do you want to be
there with him?"

Scout smiled as she let out a
light sigh. "I do. I love him. I miss
him so much."

Katherine grinned as she crossed
her arms against her chest
triumphantly. "That's what I
thought."

"He's my person," Scout said
relieved. She shrugged. "For better
or worse."

"I love that," Katherine said. She
walked over and looped her arm
around Scout's as they walked to
the dining room.

"You know, Scout, R.J. and I
never got married because we
didn't want to," Katherine said.
"We knew we loved each other and
that's all we needed."

"I know." Scout smiled at her as they sat down at the clean, white dining room table. Katherine took Scout's hand.

"But both of us had been married before," Katherine said. "Then, R.J. lost the love of his life to a car crash. I lost mine to cancer. And we felt incredibly lucky to find love after that."

Scout nodded as tears struck her eyes. Josh was the love of her life. She couldn't even imagine the immense pain Katherine or R.J. must have felt after their respective tragedies.

"I've had marriage and no marriage." Katherine shrugged. "Both lives have been unbelievably fulfilling. So, whatever path you choose with Josh, it will be fine, I

promise you. All that matters, is
that it's with Josh."

Scout felt a beautiful warmth
spread across her chest. Katherine
was right, of course. It wouldn't
matter what she and Josh chose to
do. It only mattered that they chose
their life together.

"Katherine, will you help me
with something?"

Katherine perked up with a
smile. "Do I get to be part of a
scheme? Jaime and Lucas do them
all the time, and I want to play,
too."

Scout laughed as she squeezed
Katherine's hand. "You do get to be
part of a scheme. A really, really
good one."

Scout winked at her.

"Better than Jaime and Lucas's?" Katherine asked with an eyebrow raise.

"Way better."

Katherine grinned. "Then count me in."

Scout smiled as relief washed over her. She knew exactly what to do next to win back Josh and get their relationship on track.

She couldn't wait to make it happen. She only hoped Josh was on the same page as her this time around.

**19**

## Guess Who Came for Dinner?

Josh absentmindedly adjusted his comfy T-shirt as he walked into his father's office and sat down across from him at his desk.

"I haven't sat at your desk since I was twelve," Josh said. He casually crossed his hands in front of him as his jeans crinkled.

"A mistake," R.J. lamented as he took a sip of his whiskey. "You should have been sitting here instead of Double Digits."

"Knock it off," Josh said. He grinned. "I was never gonna run your company."

"I know," R.J. said. He sat back in his chair and took off his reading glasses, tossing them on the desk.

"And I'm damn proud of you anyway."

"Thanks."

"You doin' okay?" R.J. asked. His father's look of genuine concern made Josh smile. They had come so far since Pappy's death. Pappy would like that something good had come out of it. He would think it was efficient and "about damn time."

"I am," Josh said. He nodded his head. "Whatever Scout decides, I'm ready to make it happen. I love her. Married or not married. Kids or no kids. She's it for me."

"Good," R.J. said. He nodded, pride emanating from his eyes. "I'm glad you found someone like that. Your mother was that to me."

"You really loved her, didn't you?" Josh asked.

"Oh, son, we had a love like no other," R.J. said. He dropped his hands on the desk and leaned toward Josh, his white shirt sleeves rolled up to his elbows. "She had this way about her. No one, and I mean no one else could make me feel like that."

"Scout's like that," Josh said quietly. He flicked at a nonexistent thread on his jeans as he contemplated how much he truly loved her. He looked back to R.J.

"I know. I've seen it on your face," R.J. said. "Scout is like me, huh? And you…you're like your mom."

Josh nodded his head. "Well, Scout's nicer than you, but yeah,

you're similar. Steady. Decisive.
Logical."

"And you're like your mom.
Wild, creative, emotional."

A silence swept between them.

"Your mom would love Scout,
Josh," R.J. said knowingly. "She
really would."

"Jaime, too," Josh said.

"Yep," R.J. said. "She'd be so
proud of you boys."

"Yeah, I think she would, too."

R.J. let out a held sigh as he
clapped his hands. "Should we
eat?"

"Sure, yeah," Josh said. He
crinkled his forehead and looked at
his watch. "Where's Katherine? It's
Christmas Eve. We always have
dinner early."

"Yeah, I don't know, she said
she had an errand to run or
something," R.J. commented
cagily. "Let's see if she's back."

Josh stood and headed for the
door as R.J. followed him out of
the office. They walked down to
the festively decorated dining room
where Lucas and Jaime were
already seated at the candlelit table.
Jaime had tears in her eyes.

"What's wrong?" Josh asked as
R.J. came up behind him and gave
him a slap on the back.

Josh glanced around as
Katherine appeared from around
the corner, followed by Scout's
mom and dad.

"Oh my goodness, hey," Josh
said surprised. He walked over and

hugged each of them tight. "Merry Christmas, it's so good to see you."

"You, too, Josh," Scout's mother said.

"Yeah, Merry Christmas, Josh," Scout's father said.

"I don't understand, why are you here?" he asked.

"Josh," Scout said.

When Josh turned around, Scout was on one knee in front of him, holding a gold wedding band.

His eyes misted over at the sight of her. This was the Christmas miracle he had hoped for and was now in front of him.

The only thing he wanted for Christmas, was Scout.

## 20

## This is New

Josh couldn't hold back the grin that was slathered on his face as he stared down at his beautiful partner and felt a surge of warmth and love fill his body.

Scout was here. In Pittsburgh. A Christmas miracle. The fact she was holding a wedding band was the icing on the cake.

"Scout." Josh whispered as a desperate rush of happiness filled his soul.

"Josh, I love you," Scout said. Tears filled her jade-green eyes, dark now in the candlelight, as her long, dark hair tumbled down over her V-cut red top. The look showed off her stunning curves.

"Baby," he said quietly. "I love you, too."

She smiled as her tears slid over the edges of her eyes and down her cheeks. He reached down and gently wiped them off with his thumbs.

"I want to marry you, Josh," she gushed. "I want to be your wife. I want a future together, and to figure it out…together. I want to build something as beautiful as what Paps had with Bessie. And my mom has with my dad."

His heart skipped a beat in his chest. To hear her say she wanted the same thing was almost more than he could take, and the fact she'd decided it on her own was even better.

Josh would have given Scout commitment or marriage; it wouldn't have mattered. All he wanted was for them to be on the same page. And, finally, they were. They were moving forward together, finding compromises for each other.

"Will you be my husband?" she asked.

He let out a deep sigh. He glanced around at their families staring at him, smiling, and he knew exactly what to say.

"I don't know, I'll have to think about it."

"Josh!" Scout exclaimed. He couldn't help but laugh as he was quickly joined by their families' loud cheers.

"Of course I'll marry you, get up here," he said. He helped her stand as she slipped the band on his finger. He pulled her into a deep kiss to a rousing chorus of claps and whoops.

"I love you, baby," she said.

"I love you, too."

"I'm sorry it took me a minute to get here."

"Scout, we're not always going to be in the same place at the same time," Josh said. "We just need to be honest with each other."

She nodded. "Yes, we do."

He ran his thumb lightly across her cheek.

"I should have told you about Pittsburgh," he said. "And what I wanted, too, you know? We can't think our relationship is so fragile

that we can't talk about hard things
or things we want."

"I agree," she said. "I should
have told you about the test and the
endometriosis and what it meant. I
should have had you by my side."

"Yeah," he said. They nodded at
each other and shared a light kiss.

"That's the next conversation we
need to have," she said. "Where we
want to live, children, my
endometriosis, our careers—all of
it. And then, make the decision
about next steps together."

"I like that," he said. "I'm
looking forward to that argument."

"Discussion," she corrected.

They both gave a little laugh.

"Good," she said. She slid her
hands up around his neck and
kissed him.

"We also need to, you know, plan our wedding," she said coyly.

"Oh shit, our wedding, baby," Josh said. "It's gonna be epic. Better than Lucas's."

"I heard that," Lucas shouted.

"Your wedding will not be better than ours," Jaime said competitively.

Scout lifted an eyebrow at her future sister-in-law. "Oh, bigger and better, baby."

"That's my girl!" Josh pulled Scout in for a kiss as she started laughing. He had never heard anything so sweet.

She was going to be his wife. They were going to do life together. And that's all he ever wanted.

# 21

## Moving Parts

*One year later*

Scout glanced around the empty Del Mar cottage and shook her head. The neighbors had thrown them a going-away party a few weeks ago and work had thrown her one right after. It had been the right decision for Scout to stay another year at StudioX. The discussion she and Josh had had about it was heated.

"I don't think you need it," he had said.

"It's what you think, Josh, it's what I think," she had said.

And after an hour of that back-and-forth, he had finally relented.

"If you want it and you think that's what you need, and if you're not ready to leave California yet, then we'll stay."

And they had compromised and stayed, even though Lucas hated it and complained loudly for the entire year about it.

"Enough, Lucas," Josh had finally said.

"Fine," Lucas had conceded. After that, he knocked it off, but still sent Scout random gifs or Tik-Tok videos that communicated his dissatisfaction. She had to laugh. Lucas was only doing it because he wanted them home, and that was okay with her.

Over the last month, it had been a rush to get everything ready to go and to cherish the things that they loved here one last time. She and Josh had, of course, made love at their spot by the lake, and they'd said goodbye to everyone in California they needed to.

She couldn't believe it was finally happening. They were finally moving back to Pittsburgh and starting the next chapter of their lives together. It was a beautiful dream come true. It was imperfect, crazy, wild, fun, and everything she'd ever wanted from love.

"I'm gonna miss this place," Josh said. He walked up and stood next to her with Buster right behind him. The dog sat down next to Scout and grinned up at her.

"You're gonna miss it, too, aren't you buddy?" she asked.

Buster panted and then laid down at Scout's feet.

"So many memories here," Scout said quietly.

"Yeah, great memories," Josh agreed. He slid his hand around her waist and squeezed.

"You sent an email about the basement door to the Realtor?" Scout asked.

"I did," Josh said. "He said he'll let the new owners know."

"Ugh, new owners," Scout said quietly. "It's hard to imagine anyone else living here."

"Yeah," he answered.

She leaned into his chest as they quietly looked around at the clean hardwood floors and the bright sunshine. It was hard to leave the home where they had started their relationship. Del Mar and California would always hold special places in their hearts.

"Ready for the next chapter, baby?" Josh asked. He gave her a light pat on her hips.

"I am." She turned to him and smiled. "I'm so excited to move into the Pond House. Is Lucas pissed he can't use it anymore?"

"Totally," Josh said. "I had to remind him that he got the Mustang. That helped."

She wrapped her arms around his neck as he slid his hands around her waist.

"I can't wait to get married there," she said.

"I know, right? It'll be beautiful. Spring flowers. Spring bride."

He grinned then kissed her.

"Are you excited to get the company in order over the next year?" she asked.

"I am," he said. "Are you excited to take it over in a year?"

"So excited," she breathed. "I'm glad I put in this extra year at StudioX, though. I think it really helped. I needed it."

"I get it." He kissed her again. "You're gonna be amazing, baby."

She grinned at him, then looked away.

"Hey, don't do that," he said. He gently touched her chin and pulled her face to his. "The doctor didn't say we couldn't have kids. It's not impossible."

"It's also not likely." Her eyes filled with tears.

"Hey, look at me," he said.
"We're gonna be fine. We're gonna
try, and then, if after a year we're
not pregnant, we'll try something
else. And we'll get on adoption
lists, and we'll go from there.
Okay?"

She nodded as he wiped away
the few tears that escaped her eyes.
"Okay."

"And we're godparents to Zach,
and aunt and uncle to Casey and
Zach…we have children in our
lives. Great children."

"And we are fantastic at being
the best aunt and uncle around,"
she said.

"We really are," he agreed.

"I'm so excited to babysit Zach
and Casey," she said. "I can't

believe Zach is three-months old already."

"Right? Lucas is so happy he had a son."

"The first child as a boy?" Scout rolled her eyes.

"Oh no, that's not why," Josh said.

"It isn't?"

"No, it's because Casey is a boy and he wanted them to be brothers."

Scout closed her eyes and sighed, then opened them and grinned at Josh. "Like you and him."

"Yeah," Josh said quietly.

"Ah, I like that. Makes sense."

He kissed her again. "I can't wait to go home."

"Me, too, baby, me too."

Scout exhaled a content breath
as Josh held her in their first home
together. She couldn't wait until
they were settled into their second
home, and she was his wife, for
better or worse, children or none,
and with all the love they shared
for the rest of their lives.

<u>**More to Come!**</u>

If you loved reading about Scout and Josh falling in love and want to see how their romance ends, you're in luck! Follow Scout, Josh, Lucas, and Jaime in Book 3 of the *Double Digits Pocket Romance Series*, *The Pond House*, by Author Steph West! Check out the series by scanning below.

<u>**Review this book!**</u>

Did you love *California Love*? Then let everyone know! Leave a review on Amazon by scanning below.